PRAISE FOR EDUARDO BERTI

WINNER OF THE 2011 EMECÉ PRIZE
AND 2012 LAS AMÉRICAS PRIZE FOR *The Imagined Land*

"With a very clear voice, which could pass as a translation of a Chinese text, the speaker of Eduardo Berti's *The Imagined Land* is Ling, a girl whose subjectivity strives to separate—perhaps like all oppressed subjectivities—from the mandates of an epoch."

—PAULA JIMÉNEZ, *Clarín*

"Eduardo Berti is a real innovative talent."

—PAUL BAILEY, *The Daily Telegraph*

"In this novel of learning... Eduardo Berti creates one of the most subtle feminine characters in Argentine literature. In China in the early twentieth century, a world that is torn between the ghosts of tradition and the cataclysm of modernity, an adolescent girl is initiated into the secrets and traps of love, and discovers how to find her freedom despite the yoke of social rules."

—PEDRO B. REY, *La Nación*

"Like switching on a light switch, *Agua* is as utterly simple as it is warmly illuminating... haunting quality... When a character feverishly finds herself abandoning the real world for the one of her dreams we're swept along, intoxicated with her."

—MARY ELIZABETH WILLIAMS, *New York Times Book Review*

"*Agua* meets expectations in an exquisitely roundabout fashion... This fantasy by an Argentinian delights in its journey."

—ISABEL MONTGOMERY, *The Guardian*

"A novel that can be read in a couple of evenings, very entertaining... an enjoyable story."

—MARTA MARNE, *Leer sin Prisa*

THE IMAGINED LAND

Eduardo Berti

TRANSLATED FROM THE SPANISH
BY CHARLOTTE COOMBE

DEEP VELLUM PUBLISHING
DALLAS, TEXAS

Deep Vellum Publishing
3000 Commerce St., Dallas, Texas 75226
deepvellum.org · @deepvellum

Deep Vellum Publishing is a 501c3
nonprofit literary arts organization founded in 2013.

ISBN: 978-1-941920-61-9 (paperback) • 978-1-941920-62-6 (ebook)
Library of Congress Control Number: 2017938736

—

Cover design & typesetting by Anna Zylicz • annazylicz.com
Text set in Bembo, a typeface modeled on typefaces cut by Francesco Griffo for Aldo Manuzio's printing of *De Aetna* in 1495 in Venice.
Distributed by Consortium Book Sales & Distribution.
Printed in the United States of America on acid-free paper.

To Héctor Bianciotti.

To Baoyan Zhao, for her help.

To Mariel and to Ulises, more than ever.

The ultimate elegance: the imagined land.

'MRS. ALFRED URUGUAY,' WALLACE STEVENS

XIAOMEI

The new sun illuminated the first day of the new year. We had been awake all night, as was customary on the *danian-ye*. Then at dawn, we had devoted the first hours—the hours of the long shadows—to visiting our dearest neighbours to wish them a good year, or at least a better year than the one just gone. Many of them gave us a gift of two small cloth bags, each containing a coin—one for my brother, one for me—and all of them wished the same thing to my father: for grandmother's death to bring peace to the heart of the family and to ward off any other deaths.

When the first sun of the new year reached its highest point in the sky, it did not find us unprepared. Outside our house, in the courtyard half-shaded by an awning, we had laid out the objects ready for the light of the *chu-yi*. There were mattresses and tablecloths for the sun's rays to caress, and also the oldest books, the ones with pages as yellowed as autumn leaves, so that the first wind, the first air of the new year would purify them and prevent them from deteriorating by chasing away any insects living among their pages. According to my father, the insects preferred certain words and knew how to seek them out in the oldest books, until they had devoured them. Many of the neighbouring families used to mock these old beliefs and ancient rituals. They thought them obsolete and ineffective; but my parents were very superstitious, my father more so than my mother, and his adherence to tradition seemed to have re-intensified since grandmother's death.

That day, my father put my brother and me in charge of selecting the books and carrying them outside, while my mother was busy draping sheets over a length of bamboo cane. She hung up not just the ones we had been using on the final day of the year, but also all the folded sheets stored in cupboards, and Li Juangqing (who was more than simply a cook, but not quite a governess) followed suit with the four or five tablecloths we owned.

At the time, it seemed logical to me that we only owned white fabrics, but now that decades have passed, I wonder what compulsion prevented us from covering the beds and tables of our home with any other colour. I like to think that the books made up for the lack of colour, the classic editions discreetly bound in solemn leather in measured hues of emerald green or cherry red, sky blue, grey, or ochre. I liked the contrast of the sheets and tablecloths strung up, with the books piled up beneath them. My brother, however, could not get on with books at all: he lacked that blend of dedication and curiosity required to be a good reader. Or perhaps it was the turbulent age he was at, which prevented him from sitting down and applying himself to reading. My brother was seventeen; I was coming up for fourteen. My brother's blood was pulsing in a way I could not yet comprehend, but which fascinated me, the way one is mesmerised watching the choppy waves of a raging sea.

After grandmother died, my father forbade us from going into her bedroom. No blood relatives were allowed to enter her room until forty-nine days had passed since her death. There were still sixteen days to go until they lifted the veto, and, as every six days my father would oblige us to hold a ceremony with the aim of banishing the soul of the dead woman, there were still two ceremonies left to go.

In the meantime, Li Juangqing was allowed to go into the room to clean. I confess that I was relieved to be forbidden from going in: my grandmother had suffered a long agony and I was the one who had to attend to her in her final moments. I could not shake the image from my head. It had all happened right there, in the bed we were still calling her deathbed. My grandmother had been ill for too long; I could not say since when exactly, but I remember that many things had happened while she was shrinking away beneath the bed sheets, becoming weaker and more wrinkled, the pain gradually eating away at her. The day my father brought a rabbit home, my grandmother was laid up in bed. The day the rabbit escaped and we had to turn the house upside down until we found it inside my father's left boot, my grandmother was still in bed. The night when my brother had a kind of nightmare, took a few steps like a sleepwalker and chipped half of his tooth by colliding with a door, my grandmother was still alive but had worsened considerably. I could list ten or maybe twelve episodes that I associate with my grandmother dying, as she lay face up on that bed.

Why was I the one, at the meagre age of thirteen, in charge of looking after her? There were a number of reasons: because my grandmother and Li Juangqing had never seen eye to eye; because my brother was going through a turbulent time as I have mentioned, and my father and mother did not view him as a very reliable nurse; because my father worked incessantly and was not at home very often; because I am a woman, and it is preferable to have a woman looking after a sick old lady who was frequently in a state of undress. My mother had originally been the one assigned to looking after her, and was probably doing it most efficiently, until she made a mistake. Thinking that my grandmother was asleep, she told a visiting friend that her mother was not actually sick, but just old. My grandmother overheard her and took grave offence. She forbade her from entering her room, or rather, from going in there on her own. Since my mother was the one who fed, cleaned, and attended to her needs, including massaging her back and feet (tasks she was very skilled at), my presence was required. I was like a key that my mother needed in order to step over the threshold.

I do not think my grandmother ever forgave my mother for not viewing her as ill, and she died with that resentment in her heart. We talked about it once, out of earshot of everyone else. My grandmother was not in denial about her old age. Of course not. She did, however, defend the right to feel ill.

I have the same rights as a young woman, don't I? she asked, nodding in agreement at her own words, not really caring about my opinion on the matter.

As the death of my grandmother drew nearer (we could all see it coming, although we did not know when, or wish to talk about it), my mother pulled further away from her and my father drew closer. During an intermediate stage, in a period of transition that lasted a couple of weeks, I found myself alone for the first time with this woman, who was still my father's mother and had lately started to show, due to her dramatic weight loss, a jaw that was identical to her son's.

In the final three weeks with my grandmother, everything we did was reduced to a kind of exercise that I had recently initiated; a sort of mental gymnastics to prevent her memory from stagnating. What's your son called, grandmother? I would ask. What's your brother's name? She always answered correctly, although sometimes after a concerted effort, and sometimes with a look that seemed to say, but isn't my brother dead? Or, but my son's still alive, isn't he? Maybe it was unwise of me to mix up the living and the dead, but then again, this was the same woman who just a few years ago used to regale me with a repertoire of at least thirty ghost stories.

The day came when my grandmother answered the question about her brother's name incorrectly. This happened the following day, and the day after. Not long after that came the day when she could not answer any of the questions correctly. That day she also did something unexpected. She asked me to open a drawer and pass her a tiny object wrapped in a rectangle of red silk. I did as I was told. It seemed for all the world—and it was impossible not to conclude as such—as if I were carrying out her final wishes. She unfolded the silk with trembling hands.

This is yours and always has been, she said, looking me straight in the eye.

It was a collar, also red. I immediately understood: it was the rabbit's collar. The rabbit that one day had hidden itself away in my father's boot and that, weeks later, had disappeared from the house without a trace. My brother said that my father had killed the rabbit to give the meat to his friend Gu Xiaogang. I remember going to my father and asking him if this was true (without letting on that the information had come from my brother). He immediately denied it. Yet a day later, Li Juangqing made another remark to the same effect. Now my grandmother, dusting off the collar, seemed to be tipping the balance to the detriment of my father.

Concerned that all the signs seemed to be pointing to one thing—what with her forgetting names and then suddenly remembering the collar—I decided to talk to my mother. To my amazement, she barely batted an eyelid. A doctor had visited at midnight while my brother and I were sleeping and told them that grandmother had only hours left to live.

Unusually for him, my father stayed at home that day. In the morning he shut himself away to work. In the afternoon, at almost the exact moment it started to rain, my mother and I undressed grandmother and dressed her again in clean clothes, ready for death. We then went to look for my father. Grandmother was delirious, or something like that. My father appeared with my brother and we spent a long time in silence, while the pattering rain seemed to speak to the dying woman in a secret language; a language as secret as the one she had taught me unbeknownst to my parents and my brother.

With my grandmother only minutes away from death, my father whisked her pillow away and swiftly left the room.

My mother did not follow him. She looked at my brother, then smiled at me. We had not dared to move. She explained to us that grandmother needed to depart peacefully. She had to be in a straight, horizontal position. A dying person should also never be able to see their feet. This was something my grandmother always used to say in her ghost stories.

As for the pillow—the one she had rested her head on during her long agony, but which had not received her final breath—it remained on our sloping roof for months afterward, pinned down with a few nails to stop the wind from blowing it away so that the birds could peck at it, as was traditional. The pillow relentlessly decayed and—along with the sheets, tablecloths, and books—fell victim to the brilliant warmth of the first sun.

She asks me why I have come. I reply that I am slightly worried.

About me? she says.

No, I explain. Your future is the least of my worries. What worries me is your brother.

Then she tells me she does not understand why I am visiting her, and that perhaps I would be better off visiting his dreams.

I tell her that I am not free to choose, that I go wherever I am called.

And your brother is busy dreaming about other things, I say, laughing.

But I didn't summon you.

Of course you did! I say loudly. There's no doubt about that, and anyway, I admit, I wanted to see you.

See me? she says. But I can't see you, and that's not fair.

The one who dreams is the one who sees, isn't that the way it should be?

I feel like I should clarify that there is a mistake in there. The one who is dreamed about is the one who sees. The one who dreams thinks they have seen something, but they only think that because of the images their mind creates when they wake up.

There is a silence, and as she has no proof of my existence apart from my voice, she asks me to say something.

Without hesitation, I tell her I miss her. Then I ask her to tell me the same thing.

I miss you, she says. Are you going to come often?

I don't know, because it's not up to me. I'll come when you summon me, that's for sure, and while this is still unresolved.

This? she asks. Your bird? My brother?

I do not answer.

Grandmother, are you there? Grandmother?

Although I try, I cannot be completely silent. I know she can hear the rasping sound of my breathing.

On the first day of the new year, my father was in such a good mood that he was hardly recognisable; he was usually so moderate, so restrained. He saw that there was sun, that the air was fresh, and there was no threat of clouds on the horizon, or the 'corner of the sky' as my grandmother used to call it. This all seemed to be a good omen, since nothing was more desirable for the *chu-yi* than a crystal clear dawn. Shortly after, at midday, he reminded us enthusiastically that in the evening we would be joined for dinner by the family of his friend Gu Xiaogang, who lived about a two-hour drive away by car from our city. This was a dangerously ambiguous distance: not far enough to justify the months that had passed since his last appearance, but not near enough for him to visit us regularly, which would have suited my father, as he was always finding excuses to avoid travelling to see his friend.

Gu Xiaogang was a civil servant, although he also had a reputation as a poet: a reputation based on some love poems that he had composed when he met his wife. That was the official explanation, at least. The book, his only book, had been published after his wedding. Mother used to recite a few verses from it. The verses compared his wife's eyes to the reflection of the moonlight in the bottom of a well filled with water. Other poems alluded to lips, hair or eyebrows, to legs, hands or feet. The descriptions rarely bore any similarity to the appearance of Mrs Gu; as a result, rumour had it that the poem had in fact been written for a former lover.

Gu Xiaogang's wife was considered ugly, at least by my mother and Li Juangqing, not because she was all that unattractive, but more because she did not live up to the beauty described in her husband's poem or the image of beauty that it portrayed. In addition to this, Gu Xiaogang's three daughters (he had no sons and had resigned himself to that fact) were unattractive: neither beautiful nor kind. The opposite of the merchant Liu Feihong's daughter, who in my eyes was the perfect embodiment of femininity.

Each of Gu Xiaogang's daughters had been born slightly more beautiful than the one before. The youngest, however, who was four or five years younger than me, was far from beautiful. Men like to claim that women become more beautiful by surrounding themselves by attractive friends, sisters or even daughters. I think that, in reality, the same goes for men, but for Mrs Gu it had the opposite effect: she grew uglier thanks to her offspring, and her determination to dress her daughters up elegantly—especially the eldest, known as Mulan within her clan—was also a last-ditch attempt at self-esteem.

My father wanted to marry off the eldest of these three daughters to my brother, and soon. He was sure that Gu would accept out of loyalty, despite the differences in our families' social standing. My father had dropped various hints and now they just needed to have a formal conversation. He thought that a dinner would be the perfect excuse for them to seal the deal. My brother's opinion was not relevant, and Mulan's even less so. Neither did it matter that they were both adolescents. Norms at that time were so different that I sometimes find it hard to believe that I spent my childhood in what now seems like another country, another world, rather than simply another era. As for my thoughts at the time, I am not sure what dismayed me more: my father's pig-headedness, my mother's meekness, the bovine resignation of my brother, or the certainty that the same thing would be happening to me sooner or later. They would set some unknown man before me—or more accurately, some young man—and they would impose him on me as my husband.

At that time, it was not unusual for a person unrelated to the two families to arrange the wedding. Intermediaries charged rates that were proportional to the complexity of the task, particularly when there was a certain incompatibility between the social hierarchy or economic situation of one family clan and another. My father, however, was indifferent to all of that. Mr Gu was a good friend and not even the slightest mediation would be necessary. With regards to the—as my mother saw it, contentious—issue that Gu Xiaogang's social standing had recently been elevated quite considerably, meaning that my brother could represent a step down for Mulan, my father would not let anybody mention it. It would mean admitting that his friend had a more successful career (he was a higher ranking civil servant than my father), which was a fact that his professional envy prevented him from considering or, at least, saying out loud.

It was obvious that my mother was pessimistic about the union my father wanted for my brother, but that she did not dare oppose it because Gu was liked by the family and, above all, because in our house it was my father who made those kinds of decisions.

My father was so nervous about Gu Xiaogang's impending visit, planned for the evening of the first day of the year, that when it was our turn to place the tablecloths, sheets, and old books out in the sun, he came up to my brother, scrutinised the tall mountain of offerings behind him, then did the same with my mountain of books, which was considerably lower but much sturdier. He angrily demanded to know where grandmother's books were. My brother and I stood there gaping at him. We did not know what to say.

Grandmother's books? How could we go and get them when we were forbidden from entering her room?

There was no point in my brother daring to whisper this objection. My father grumbled under his breath, looking at my mother for support.

My children are clearly stupid, I have been given stupid children, he seemed to be saying to himself.

It was true that my grandmother's oldest books were not there, in particular two volumes that she had revered when she was alive: the ghost stories of Ji Yun, which tell the story of an empty room that catches on fire spontaneously, and the wonderful stories of Gan Bao, full of human heads that fly around at night while the rest of the body is asleep or even dreaming peacefully.

My father, who believed in flying heads about as much as he believed in spontaneous combustion and who had frequently asked my grandmother not to stir up our imaginations, nonetheless was scared that the unforgiveable act of forgetting these books would have terrible consequences and that the new year would be even worse than the previous one.

Was I not clear when I told you to bring out all the old books, all of them? he said, raising his eyebrows.

What he had meant for us to do, apparently, was tell Li Juangqing to go into the room to choose some of grandmother's books. Of course, my father gave these orders immediately and Li Juangqing soon scurried back carrying the oldest books, or at least the most tattered. Among them was one of my favourites: *The Wood of Jests*, by Xu Zichang. I can still quote various sections of this book from memory, such as the story of the learned man who boasts about being rich and therefore draws the attention of a thief. After breaking into the man's house one night, the thief discovers that he has lied about his wealth, and runs away, angry. The learned man gives chase, catches up with the thief and begs for his forgiveness, offering him his only coin: Please, sir, accept this money and be kind enough not to tell anyone what you saw in my house.

What about this book? said my father, frowning. Where has this book come from? I don't remember having it in the house.

The Wood of Jests was wholly disrespectful according to my father's criteria. He believed in the sun ritual with the same incomprehensible fear instilled in him by the household god, whose altar he would fill with walnuts, hazelnuts, and numerous offerings to his ancestors. There was a lengthy list of dead people who required honouring, now including my recently deceased grandmother.

Although the books calmed my father down, they did not

manage to restore his cheerful mood. At lunchtime, he grumpily hurled his chopsticks down and complained that Li Juangqing had tried to cook a certain dish in a certain way, despite his instructions to cook it the way grandmother used to. He was sullen all afternoon, and even more so when Gu was late arriving. He was just in the process of scolding us again over something trivial, when we heard the sound of Gu Xiaogang's car, at first in the distance, then getting closer.

Receiving a visit from an automobile was exceptional in those days, even something to be proud of. I knew that the neighbours could also hear the sound of that engine growing louder, the unmistakable sign that a car was coming. All of them would be asking themselves the same thing: Whose house was it going to? My father had told us yesterday, at our New Year's Eve dinner, that his friend Gu bought a car and has promised to take us out for a spin in it. Knowing this beforehand, unlike our neighbours, knowing for certain that we were the privileged ones,was like knowing how the dice will fall while you are still rattling them in your fist.

When the car finally pulled up right in front of our house beneath the curious gaze of all the neighbourhood children and several adults, we were perplexed to see only one passenger getting out of the car. It was Mr Gu; no wife or children with him. It did not take my father long to realise that the marriage arrangement was in jeopardy. He gestured for all of us, apart from my mother, to keep to one side while he greeted his friend. Like in one of those silent movies that I used to love so much (I thought I knew everything about Shanghai cinema and actresses like Shan Hu, Jingxia Zhao, or Ruan Lingyu), my father and Mr Gu shook hands somewhat ostentatiously; their lips moved; they smiled and even pointed in unison at us, their faithful audience. Then my father and his friend shut themselves away in the study that my father used very occasionally. My mother promptly ordered Li Juangqing to prepare tea and asked my brother and me to escort her to the terrace, so she could help us take down the tablecloths and sheets and carry the books back to their shelves. Or rather, to the door of the forbidden room so that Li Juangqing could put them back in their places later. I now realise that she used to invent things to keep us occupied, to ease the tension of waiting.

We did not manage to complete our chores; we had barely dismantled the piles of books when my father reappeared, alone, without Mr Gu, and in the background we heard the sound of the engine, but going the other way, slowly fading. The sound of the engine disappearing into the distance meant more than just Gu Xiaogang leaving: with it went our chance to ride in the car. My father looked drained and ghostly, like a melancholy scarecrow that had suddenly popped up on our terrace. Either the meeting had been very short, or we had taken an abnormally long time to fold the sheets.

All the while, my father stood there with a look on his face that I had never seen before. He was staring at the books onto which he had projected all his hopes and fears. Only now he was looking at them as if he were seeing them for the first time, unable to attribute a purpose to them, summoning up the strength to overcome this defeat.

Several days passed before we finally found out the details of the conversation between my father and his friend Gu. Naturally, my father had gotten ahead of himself before fully consulting Gu Xiaogang and had constructed an imaginary palace in the air for the supposed marriage of my brother and Mulan.

It was hard for Mr Gu to turn down the offer, but he did so with brazen elegance. First he complimented my brother, and then my father's entire family; after that he pursed his lips, placed his fist on the wooden table that served as a desk and explained that his wife had just accepted a convenient offer to marry off not only Mulan, but also the two younger daughters: Baoyan and Baojuan. The husbands-to-be were the three sons of a prosperous merchant who was apparently very taken with Gu Xiaogang's daughter. So taken, in fact, that if he had happened to have a fourth son, he would almost have gone as far as asking Gu Xiaogang to father another daughter. The triple wedding had been agreed upon the week before, Mr Gu told my father, pulling a dismayed face again, even though—in my father's opinion—his friend's use of the word 'convenient' and the gleam in his eye contradicted any trace of regret on his face.

In those days it was quite a feat to arrange a marriage in only seven days, since a series of phases—most of them obligatory—had to be fulfilled. In Mr Gu's case, he and his wife had received a visit from the *mei-po*, representing the parents of the groom, or rather, the grooms. Having accepted the proposal after a day of reflection (Mr and Mrs Gu had not wanted to say 'yes' straight away), the merchant then appeared on the second day. The ever-present mediator had written down on a piece of paper the information relating to the six brides and grooms: the year, month, day, and even hour of their births, to be given to the fortune-teller, the *suangming xiansheng*, who would study it and put forth the arguments for and against each union. Once this was done, they let three days pass. If a misfortune or a bad omen occurred within that time, anything from the death of a dog or other pet to the illness of a distant relative, either of the two families could renounce the marriage. Nothing of that sort happened, however, and on the fifth day the *mei-po* confirmed the date of the weddings. At the adviser's suggestion, according to Gu Xiaogang, the weddings would be celebrated under the crescent moon, but on separate dates: first the oldest couple, involving Mulan, then a month later the wedding of Baoyan, and the following month that of Baojuan. It was said to be impossible to arrange a wedding in just seven days, but in this case, they had arranged three in just six days. On the seventh day, instead of resting, Mr Gu had visited the merchant's house and met his sons-in-law, which was equivalent to blessing the engagements.

According to my calculations, my father went on to tell the story of his meeting with Gu Xiaogang almost a thousand times throughout his life, and not once did I ever see him deviate from the truth (or from the first version that my family accepted as the truth). He would dig out that story not only when someone mentioned marriage agreements, but also when the conversation turned to the subject of broken friendships, betrayal, and deceit at the hands of people one knows, or how even the most honest of men can be blinded by money. There were moments when I thought that the sole purpose of my father's social life was to wait poised, like a cat, for the perfect moment to leap in with the story of his final meeting with his friend Gu Xiaogang.

The situation was troubling because the only person who was angry and sad about it was my father. The rest of my family was struggling with other emotions. My mother's pride had been wounded by Gu's refusal and she could not forgive the absence of his wife, who in her eyes had lacked the 'guts' to accompany her husband. At the same time, she knew of at least ten or twelve young women who were suitable, more beautiful, and more agreeable than Gu Xiaogang's daughter. My brother could not care less; to my utter astonishment, everything that went on within the family bored him because he seemed to be discovering an infinitely more fascinating world outside our home. However, it was an undeniable relief for him not to have to marry Mulan because, if we looked at all the potential candidates (and by potential I am talking about the young, single daughters of my father's numerous acquaintances, or at best, acquaintances of those acquaintances), Mulan was the least beautiful and interesting of the lot. I do not mean to say that such a rich selection would necessarily guarantee one of the two things that I considered ideal at the time (for my brother to choose a woman he could feasibly fall in love with, or that among the candidates there might be at least one who compared to the daughter of the blind man Liu Feihong), but my mother felt that it was not foolish to hope.

As for me, even though I shared my brother's relief and much of my mother's hope, I was troubled by my father's disappointment. Especially because the ever-attentive Li Juangqing began asking me to behave better, since my father was experiencing what she called a 'special moment.' Every moment in life is, in one way or another, special, but there are decisive events, ones which alter how we see the world and how the world sees us. Gu's refusal had damaged something more than a potential nuptial agreement: my father's firm childhood friend had rejected him in other ways, even if that had not been his intention.

Just like Mr Gu, my father worked as a civil servant, only his job was an insignificant position in a small town and, unlike his friend who had bought a car and could allow himself the luxury of turning down a candidate for his daughter, the best he could hope for was to keep his job and feel fortunate to have it. My father was not only baffled by his friend Mr Gu, who had not—in honour of their childhood memories—made the slightest effort to conceal or even play down the inequalities between the families, but he was also baffled by himself. He had not dared ask his friend why he had not told him about the triple engagement before; or why he had not asked the merchant for a longer period of reflection; or if he felt sorry to be losing my brother as a son-in-law; or, finally, why he came on his own just to deliver this news and then promptly fled like a thief in the night.

I was too young then to gauge the scope of what had happened, but not too young to notice that Mr Gu had left on the first day of the new year without saying goodbye to the rest of my family and without honouring his promise to eat with us and take us out in his car. My father's severity, coupled with the particular sadness he was displaying at the time, forced me to keep quiet although I was dying of curiosity to know if Gu Xiaogang would come to visit us again, either with or without his wife and daughters. Soon I was certain that something serious had gone on in the study that day. How else can you explain the fact that we never received invitations to any of the three weddings?

As well as feeling sorry for my father, I was also afraid. I had a guilty sense of certainty that, at any moment, my father would accuse my brother and me, perhaps even my mother too, of having caused this disgrace because we did not put my grandmother's books out in the sun. At least not the right ones. I later discovered, however, that my father attributed what had happened to another reason: for a wedding agreement to be sealed, three years must have passed since the death of a parent or grandparent (in this case, my grandmother's death), but my father had dared to violate this tradition just to please my mother. She had been set on the idea of my brother getting married before he turned eighteen, or at most, nineteen. My father had relented and was regretting it.

Marrying off my brother became, in short, my parents' main obsession; out of pride and necessity but also—as I already mentioned—because my mother thought that he was getting a bit old. My father did not agree with the latter (he had married my mother just after he turned twenty), but he did not object, because all he wanted was to find a beautiful daughter-in-law as soon as possible, one who would not only make Gu Xiaogang squirm with envy, but even more so Gu Xiaogang's wife. He saw her as the true author of the betrayal, and this gave him the perfect reason to exonerate his friend (it was not Gu who was bad, rather it was due to the poisonous influence of his wife). It also made him feel superior to Gu (Gu Xiaogang's wife tells him what to do, but in my house, I give the orders). This served as a feeble consolation for his wounded pride.

If my father had been looking for a wife for my brother, instead of the finest wife, he could have found her in the blink of an eye. The country was becoming militarised; many young men were already dying in the skirmishes with the Japanese army. Although the war was still a long way off, both in terms of time and distance, some of the neighbouring families' sons had decided to enlist. Many of them used this as an excuse to escape their old-fashioned or oppressive families. As a result, there were two or three women to every single man. This disparity was likely to increase because of what many called the 'female tide,' the rising birth rate of women. It was futile for parents to resort to such legendary methods as, for example, giving women men's names. Perhaps nature or the gods—which some people, I know, believe to be the same thing—were sending future mothers to balance out the soldiers who were soon to die.

Time passed quickly, much to the anguish of my mother, who every so often would put forward the name of another young woman and watch my father immediately rule her out. My father was on the verge of becoming an expert at saying 'no' and, like all experts, he used varied and compelling arguments, each one with crushing simplicity. The dangerous thing, which my mother soon came to realise, was that he increasingly came to enjoy this role of impugner, as if parodying his friend Gu Xiaogang on a large scale. With every candidate that he ruled out—and I cannot deny that many of them deserved a firm refusal—my father was healing the wounds caused by Gu's rejection. The candidates had no idea that my father had disapproved of them (and the parents of the candidates knew even less), since the whole process was confined to a hypothetical game. It began with my mother suggesting a specific name and ended with my father ruling the girl out, time after time.

While not giving up on proposing further candidates, my mother was despairing and often let off steam by talking to Li Juangqing. I tried not to miss these chats, which were my main source of information; although Li Juangqing usually filled me in—never my brother—on what was bothering my mother.

It took a colossal effort to stop myself from telling Li Juangqing or my mother that I had already found the dream girl for my brother. This was of course the daughter of Liu Feihong, the blind man who sold all kinds of birds at the market closest to our house. By that, I mean live birds, not the chickens, ducks, partridges, or other poultry sold at several places nearby.

Liu Feihong's daughter was the most exquisite creature I had ever seen in my life, but even so, she was not ideal—and never would be—for my father because she was poor, very poor, like the perfect heroine in a tragic novel. Her mouth, her nose, her eyes, her neck, her hands, her arms were perhaps nothing out of the ordinary if you assessed them individually—like in Gu Xiaogang's poem, almost as an examination of beauty; yet the sum of the parts was nothing short of miraculous and was helped, I now think, by the suggestive curve of her eyebrows and the unusual colour of her skin, which was neither yellowish nor typically Western, but the colour of the moon.

Today when I try to recall that face with its brilliantly whitish complexion, images of the actress Ruan Lingyu come to mind, all of them without exception in black and white, because Liu Feihong's daughter looked like she had stepped out of one of those old movies full of creatures with lunar skin. There was a difference, however. At that time, there were coloured photographs of Ruan Lingyu and other famous actresses in circulation. The original black-and-white photos were carefully painted over, particularly on the lips and the cheeks. I do not deny that the retouching did more justice to the real appearance of each actress, but it also spoiled the magic and, in my opinion, the 'real' Ruan Lingyu (even in artificial colours) was much less striking than the 'artificial' one in black and white.

Nothing like that could happen with Liu Feihong's daughter. She had such a fabulously authentic paleness that, between a black-and-white photograph of her and her real image, the only discrepancy would be in her clothing, not the colour of her skin. Did this mean that the blind man's daughter was more beautiful than Ruan Lingyu?

Nowadays, with joyful subjectivity, I could speculate that she was. She genuinely possessed what Ruan Lingyu or other actresses achieved artificially (I am talking about black-and-white cinema, but also about rice powder). Ruan Lingyu was also at the height of her beauty—by the way, who was to predict that a couple of years later she would commit suicide?—while without any makeup at all, Liu Feihong's daughter was showing the very first glimmer of her splendour. In time she would become even more beautiful.

I might have reasoned that if I liked Liu Feihong's daughter so much and she was so poor, then there was nothing to lose by mentioning her in the presence of my parents. With nothing to lose, what harm was there in putting her name on the list of candidates that my father mercilessly ripped apart? The answer is just that: I did not want her to be yet another name on any list, even less for my father to blithely dispatch her in the offhand way he had already dismissed dozens of girls.

My father's decisions and opinions had always been sacred to me, even when what he decreed prevented me from doing what I wanted. When that happened I would get angry, protest loudly, or retreat into silent hostility, but I never questioned my father's power. If anything cracked, it was my will (my 'impulsiveness' as my mother would say, springing to my father's defence, as she nearly always did) and under no circumstances his sacred authority. However, at that moment, months after Gu's final visit, seeing my father taking so much delight in rejecting young women started to have an unexpected effect on me: for the first time I was aware of his humanity; for the first time I understood the fragility and frailty behind so much of what he did. In that context, the simple idea of putting forward the blind man's daughter was almost a sacrifice. My father saying 'no' to her would be the same as—if not worse than—him rejecting me.

What is the most valuable object in the world? she wants to know.

A dead blackbird, I say.

A dead blackbird? she replies. And how many gold taels is that worth?

Exactly, I say. Nobody can tell you the price of it, and that is why it's invaluable.

She remembers a story I told her once. I must have told her about two hundred stories, but I have forgotten all of them.

I am touched by the fact that now it is the other way around; now she is telling me something in the darkness, making my words her own.

A blackbird happens upon a palace and the nobleman who lives there entertains him with the finest music and the finest wine. The blackbird, despite all of this, is sad and bemused. Obliged to do so by the nobleman, he drinks a few drops of the wine and does not dare to miss a note of the raucous music. Days later, the blackbird is found dead in the palace gardens. What happened? The nobleman does not understand. A wiseman gives him a simple explanation: You entertained the blackbird as you would have liked to be entertained, but not as the blackbird would have liked.

I met Liu Feihong and his daughter two or three days after my grandmother's death. It was before the twenty-fourth day of the last moon, when the portrait of the household god is burned and replaced by another to last the next year. It was usually my grandmother who burned the portrait, with the same conviction with which she assiduously wrote a message for my grandfather (her dead husband) and set it on fire to send it to the afterlife. To the imagined land. This is what she used to call death.

My grandmother had a white blackbird that she kept in a cage with thick iron bars and a kind of wire mesh over it. Like other elders in the city—many of whom were friends from the past—some mornings my grandmother went to the shores of a lake where you would always see birds that were bright yellow in colour except for their black heads and tails. She went there with her blackbird, as did hundreds of elders from the city or even from neighbouring villages. They took the opportunity to sit and warm themselves in the sun.

Seeing her shuffling along, watching her leaving the house carrying the birdcage, filled me with tenderness and admiration. My grandmother was no longer physically fit and I was astonished that she undertook those pilgrimages when her feet (unlike mine) had been deformed by being bound as a child. They were so disfigured that, on the one and only occasion when she dared to show them to me, they reminded me of mutilated hands. But my grandmother had learned to live on these feet and, taking reasonable breaks, she never went more than two weeks without taking her cage down to the lake.

Fortunately, her blackbird did not weigh much and the cage was portable and light, unlike those who showed off their obese birds in cages bordering on ostentatious. The cages said more about the old people than the birds did: there were cages made of iron or wire, bamboo or various kinds of wood; they were stripped or decorated, round or square; they had hooks that were twisted, long or short, some were practical to carry, others not so much...

The wisest of them preferred wooden cages, and an ebony cage was not the same as a rosewood one, because the choice was dependent on crucial details: the size or shape of the bird's wings, for example, or even the sound of the bird's song.

The variety of cages could be best appreciated when they were all hanging from the branch of a tree next to the lake, with all the birds inside, almost all of them covered by a blue cloth.

The excursions to the lake had a clear purpose: so that the bird (the white blackbird, in my grandmother's case) would sing better every day or, at least, so that it would not stop singing. There were two favoured methods for achieving this. The first involved rowing around the lake in a hired boat, with the cage on your lap. These outings were reputed to drastically improve the bird's singing. As my grandmother was no longer in any fit state to row (there were some old people who did, with the cage balanced on their knees), occasionally my father would accompany her, strengthening his arm muscles by doing the rowing. For the other method, my grandmother did not need my father or anybody else. It involved hanging the cage up with the others by the lakeside so that the birds could sing in unison, or so that in the intervening silence, the caged birds could hear the magnificent melodies of the creatures that inhabited that place: those very bright yellow birds with a splash of black. They were not only beautiful to look at but also to listen to. Among them were several 'master birds' whose primary virtue was training other birds with their fine display of warbling.

When my grandmother fell ill and had to stay in bed, her white blackbird plunged into an unyielding silence. She deduced that it was because the outings to the lake had stopped. Her doctor was opposed to her leaving her bed, and my grandmother had neither the desire nor the energy to do so. She had already completely lost the sight in her left eye and wore a patch because the light bothered her. She tried to convince herself that this was something temporary and went on smoking her only cigarette of the day at five o'clock in the afternoon as if everything were normal, but looking at her, it was impossible to believe that only a few days before she had been able to walk with the cage all the way to the lake of the singing birds and back again.

My mother, who was still speaking to my grandmother at that point, offered to take the cage to the lake. The offer came at a price for her: walking with a birdcage in our city was synonymous with old age. My mother, who was what you would call 'middle-aged,' did not know what scared her more: being rejected by the circle of old people (and not helping my grandmother) or being accepted as one of the elderly. I have come to suspect that she asked me to go with her as a way of showing that she was a mother, not a grandmother. In any case, what happened in the end was a combination of the options she dreaded: the old people received us with astonishment, but without hostility. My mother explained that she was coming on behalf of the blackbird's owner, and everyone was very sorry to hear that my grandmother had fallen ill, but at the same time, it was to be expected.

We're old, said a man who had no teeth, but still had a full head of hair. Some of us with no children or family have already appointed a guardian to take care of the bird, just in case.

Going to the lake did not have the desired result. The blackbird still refused to sing. We went two more times, but in vain. My grandmother began to worry. My father began to worry. It was Li Juangqing, who was always in the know, who told us about the blind man. She told us that at the market there was a bird seller, known as Liu Feihong, who apparently had a gift that was common among the blind (feeling the bones of the arm and foretelling the future), but who also had an extraordinary knowledge of birds. At first my mother would hear nothing of it, but soon my grandmother died and my father, affected by the ill-fated silence of the blackbird, thought that although it had been impossible to save grandmother there was no reason to give up on her bird. The mission of going to the market therefore fell to my mother; and she went with me, not with Li Juangqing, because by that point, after the excursions to the lake, we were like accomplices in the matter.

I rarely went to the market and my mother never went. It was Li Juangqing's world, the world of wood, rice, oil, and salt, as my grandmother used to call housekeeping. But that day, as my mother wanted my company and nobody else's, Li Juangqing simply drew a map for us showing the location of Liu Feihong's stall. The map was so well drawn that there was no way we could get lost.

At the market you could buy everything: porcelain wares, bottles of sweet wine, rice liqueurs, new or secondhand rugs, lemons piled high in yellow mountains, purple and red flowers, coal and firewood, eggs of all sizes, live eels, and all manner of ready-prepared dishes...

Liu Feihong's stall was not in the most accessible area, but a little farther away, close to the man who sold the strong-smelling tofu, a factor which greatly reduced the clientele around there. Nevertheless, we found him and saw that what Li Juangqing had told us was true: the blind man sold special bird feed (with milled rice, flour, and grated radish), and had cages containing all kinds of birds, from *hwameis* to parrots, from a lark to a pair of nightingales. The only birds he did not have were mythical birds, such as the *jingwei* that dreams of filling the ocean with rocks, the *dongzhen* that can distinguish lies from truth, or the *jian* that has only one eye and one wing and flies around in circles looking for its other half.

While my mother talked to the blind man, I became aware of the presence of his daughter.

I had never seen such a beautiful girl in my life. There is no room for mythical birds here, I thought. She was the only extraordinary creature.

I was thinking this when, rather abruptly, Liu Feihong unhooked a cage containing a white blackbird just like my grandmother's, albeit a little smaller.

This is what I would recommend, he said, almost in a whisper. My mother did not like what Liu Feihong was suggesting. It was like a healer prescribing an expensive medicine that only he knew how to prepare. Did we really need to buy another blackbird, and moreover, a white one? Or did Liu Feihong just want to sell us one of his rarest birds? As if reading my mother's thoughts, the blind man calmly added that he knew buying a white blackbird was not something you did every day. It was, I suppose, for the nouveau riche like Mr Gu. Not for my family. Before spending that amount we would weigh it up as if we were buying a car.

He advised her to take the blackbird for a few weeks. A sort of loan, if you will, said the blind man, and only then did I notice that his accent was from the north. If it doesn't work, Madam, bring it back to me. If it does work, pay me for those weeks and then we will see if you want to buy it or not. How does that sound? Do we have a deal?

Liu Feihong was a slip of a man who looked old before his time; but upon studying him more closely, it was easy to see that as a young man he would have had attractive features. Liu Feihong's wife, who was not blind and appeared to be about ten years younger, had an undeniable beauty, although nothing out of the ordinary. Perhaps the daughter had inherited her beauty, as is often the case, from one of her grandparents?

I could not say for sure how they concluded the negotiation. I had suddenly gone completely deaf, as if in the presence of a blind man it was only polite to lose one of your senses, and my eyes were for Liu Feihong's daughter alone. If I had been less bewildered, I would have heard her father calling her by name: Xiaomei. But I only found out this fact months later. That morning, all I could do was stare at her. I was brimming with questions whose answers I was almost glad not to know, since I felt that the mystery and the slow unveiling of each one promised to be exciting. How old was the blind man's daughter? What did her voice sound like? How did she move when she walked? How would she look with her hair tied back and her ears uncovered? While my mother negotiated a price for the bird (while she negotiated a wife for my grandmother's bird), I said to myself that here, in flesh and blood, was the perfect girl for my brother, or, without any exaggeration, the perfect girl for any young man. It was true that Xiaomei's loose-fitting dress hardly gave away anything about the shape of her body, but her wrists, her neck, the little that you could see, all implied that her body was as exquisite as her face. It was true that she was wearing shoes and you could not see if her feet had been previously bound; but Xiaomei's hands were so impossibly pale and delicate that Mr Gu would have run into serious difficulties if he had tried to devote a verse of his poetry to them.

Within a few days, and as if by magic, my grandmother's bird recovered his vocation as a singer. This made Liu Feihong's aura grow. My mother began to speak of him in the presence of my father, who uttered his name with a curious respect, as if he were a doctor or a wiseman who had healed grandmother. The fact that they were talking about Liu Feihong (and that, in the end, my family would keep the hired blackbird) meant that the existence of his daughter might also be mentioned. To my dismay, neither my mother nor Li Juangqing ever let slip that Xiaomei was attractive. Any allusion to her was only ever a fleeting or marginal remark: she was mentioned because she was the blind man's daughter; they talked about her as one might discuss an addendum, without giving her a leading role. I saw this as an unfair paradox, because as I have already said, Xiaomei looked like the actress Ruan Lingyu who was always cast as the protagonist. At the same time, I was relieved that this was how things were, for I had just made one of those discoveries, that, while unexpected, was not entirely unpleasant. Whenever my mother or father talked about the blind man, I immediately became nervous and, even worse, if the conversation turned to Xiaomei (or, strictly speaking, to four words: 'the blind man's daughter'), it was impossible to prevent my cheeks from reddening.

If someone had told me then that I was in love with Xiaomei, I would have burst out laughing. I saw her as a role model: the girl I wanted to be, and the girl I wanted at my brother's side.

I was so taken by her smile that I started practicing it in front of the mirror until I had perfected it. I am not sure if this equates to love, but as soon as we arrived home with the bird we had rented, in the cage we had bought (the blind man explained very courteously that the agreement did not include the cage), from that morning on, I started going to the market as often as I could, to see Xiaomei. I made up various excuses to offer to accompany Li Juangqing. If she did not need to go, as was sometimes the case, or if she rejected my company (because I understood later on, the market was often her alibi for her personal affairs), then I would make my own way to the market, cautiously, making sure never to go down certain streets that were reputed—and for good reason I believe—to be dangerous places for little girls.

I did not see Xiaomei every time I visited the market. Sometimes she was there with her father; other times the blind man's wife would accompany him; and less frequently, except on weekends, all three members of the family would be at the stall. Not once—at least that I had seen—was Liu Feihong absent.

When I did not get to see Xiaomei, I would return home in a bad mood. There was no doubt that the wife and daughter alternated going to the market with doing chores at home and leisure time. I was willing to pay a thousand, ten thousand gold taels to know where the family of Liu Feihong lived, to visit their house and be able to talk to Xiaomei on her own while her mother and father were working. But if I did get her on her own, what would I say to her? How could I explain my unexpected visit? I had no idea. I also had no idea if Xiaomei would recognise me if we ran into one another somewhere other than the market. Something told me that she would not, that her memory only stored the general image of my face along with Li Juangqing's face, like some strange two-headed creature that frequented the market, and she would therefore be unable to recognise us individually.

One morning at the market, a morning when Xiaomei was

not there, I overheard a banal conversation between the blind man and an old woman I had seen there before. She liked to talk to the caged birds and had made up names for nearly all of them.

Suddenly, the old woman asked where the blind man's daughter was. He replied that the girl spent her free mornings in the park, the same park containing the lake of the singing birds. Xiaomei's mother added that, just as the father was fanatical about birds, the daughter had a passion for trees and flowers.

Until that moment, I had known nothing about Xiaomei's tastes and habits. Despite how erratic she was, I had gathered that she preferred to dress in grey or dark blue, instead of colours like green, white, or pink, and that she liked to decorate the buttons of her clothing with red or yellow fabric. My devotion fed off such trivial details, but the fragility of my conclusions had already been proved: as soon as I gathered that Xiaomei preferred a certain coloured buttons, she would change them. As soon as I presumed that Xiaomei always wore her hair down, perhaps because she wanted to hide some flaw or blemish on her neck, a few days later I would see her with her hair tied up (or even in plaits like the ones I still wore), and I would conclude that no, her neck was indeed exquisite. Finding a flaw in her was harder than catching a needlefish in the sea.

Unlike my feeble guesswork, the information proffered by Liu Feihong's wife was different: it was a real, concrete fact that I could trust, and it called for courage on my part.

I no longer cared that I did not know where Liu Feihong's family lived. I no longer cared that I did not have a single miserable tael (I did not actually know what a tael was, but I found the word itself quite charming), and I cared even less about whether or not Xiaomei would recognise me. All I had to do was walk through the park, and above all else, come up with a plan to arouse Xiaomei's interest in me and justify bumping into her.

In the well-stocked library inherited from our grandmother, there was a wide variety of books, among them a volume on trees and a kind of catalogue of flowers. The books had been gathering dust for decades, but once forty-nine days had finally elapsed following the death of my grandmother, and the ban on entering her room was lifted, and I was fortunate to gain not only access to them, but access with a freedom that my grandmother would have never permitted. In life, she had acted as a combination of teacher and librarian: rationing out the books, giving them to me one at a time, in a specific order that she felt matched my growing understanding of the world. Now, with this unrestricted access, I was discovering books I did not even know existed.

It was only logical for my grandmother to be the keeper of the library, because she not only told me a story every night, but she was also in charge of teaching my brother and me to read, write, and do sums. During her illness, she had managed to carry on with the stories but not with the lessons because they made her too tired. This led to a disruption in our education. My mother then suggested that we go to school, but my father argued that the idea did not make sense: grandmother would soon be better and we could carry on our education. I doubt he really thought that. Now I realise that my father clung to traditions so tightly that he disapproved of public and mass education.

He used his faith in grandmother's very improbable recovery as a barrier against any suggestion my mother made.

She did not dare, of course, give up hope for Grandmother before my father did.

After the death of our grandmother, my mother did not insist on our going to school, and we began to receive a private tutor. He visited a couple of days a week, halfway through the afternoon. He was a man verging on old age, painfully thin, with sunken cheeks and very bad breath. When he asked me to approach him and look him in the eye, convinced that it would help me gain a better understanding of ideas I could not grasp, it was no use clenching my lips together. There was no way of neutralizing that dreadful breath.

With the help of the tireless Li Juangqing, my mother redecorated the room that had been my grandmother's bedroom to become the parlour where she did her embroidery and where the elderly teacher gave us lessons. Seeing my grandmother's bed gone, and her furniture all moved around—particularly her books—made me immensely sad, as if grandmother were dying a second time. Only later did I realise that if Grandmother was able to die a second time—at least to me—this meant that maybe she was not entirely dead, that she and I were in denial of that.

One afternoon, our teacher made the mistake of criticising the books in the room. He did not make an actual remark, he simply glanced at the hard leather spines and pursed his lips when he saw the stories of Pu Songling and the section devoted to ghost stories. The first night we were told about the teacher, my father had warned us (my brother, but more me) not to mention that our grandmother had died in that room months before. He undoubtedly feared that the teacher would be shocked or would deem it inappropriate to give us lessons in there. However, when I saw the teacher's disdainful attitude toward those books, I was on the verge of breaking the promise I had made to my father; perhaps the teacher, having snubbed the ghost stories, would tremble when he found out that the room was already inhabited by death. I imagined this with some delight and hoped that the fear would drive him away indefinitely.

As if he sensed this and was afraid of the room, our tutor gave us an unusual class the next time: he made us leave the house, took us to a quiet street, and made us run between a cherry tree on one corner and another tree in the distance, two or three times, there and back. When he saw that we were tired, he ordered us to stop and wrap our right hands around our left wrists so we could feel our heartbeat, the blood galloping through our veins.

My mother was outraged when she found out that this was our only lesson that day. Foolishly, she complained about it in front of my father, who suggested we look for a better teacher. Of course, the same thing happened as it had done with the potential brides for my brother: he never approved any other candidate, always giving a more or less valid reason, and so my mother became our sole educator.

At first, I was glad because I did not want to be visited by any other teachers (not even ones with better breath); but I longed to get out of the house and was therefore furious with my brother for not demanding to go to public school. If he had been firmer about it, my father would probably have given in, and I would have been able to go too. But my brother was not interested in studying and had enough friends—very few, but enough for him—without the need for school.

I am not sure what is more inconceivable to me now: the fact that neither of my parents seemed shocked by my brother's completely unscholarly attitude, or that my mother was the one who educated us, using methods that were far from academic. Try as I might, I cannot recall a single moment when my brother or my parents took the trouble to read one of grandmother's books. It was an unspoken fact that I was the one who had inherited those books. Even so, in a contradictory move, my mother forbade me from taking them out of the room they were in, no matter how much I explained that I would not take them far (to my bed, at most) and, above all, that they would never leave the house.

My mother seemed to forget that those books had been stacked up in the courtyard in the light of the *chu-yi*. Or had this been an exceptional occurrence, done only out of pure necessity?

For two weeks I devoted my afternoons to two activities: I walked through the park with some sheets of paper I had stolen from my father and copied onto them (I have always been terrible at drawing) the outlines of certain trees and flowers that caught my interest. Then, once back home, I consulted my grandmother's books for information. I quickly learned to tell a jasmine from an azalea, a begonia from a narcissus. I soon knew their names and they stopped being just flowers, but for some unknown reason I found it harder to remember the names of trees.

My mother took me by surprise one day, as I was engrossed in my investigations. She shook her head and murmured something that, although I did not hear it, was an expression of astonishment. I discovered that I liked those books (not just the books of poems or stories) and that I enjoyed studying flora. At the same time, I noticed how imprecise my method was. When I was reunited with my grandmother's books, the spindly drawings that had seemed so accurate in the park showed their limitations. The tree or plant I had spent half an hour drawing might have been specimen two on page twenty-six, or specimen three on page fifty, or various other options. I squinted, forgetting my drawing, until I had reconstructed the original image in my mind, and concluded that it was a particular tree. But when I saw it again the following day in the park, I was frustrated because the illustration in the book, as I remembered it, seemed to only partially correspond and there were minor details that made me doubt my conclusion.

My defeat (or my victory) was partial. I started to recognise families of trees or plants, but not specific species. Not yet.

The area of these investigations, as I have said, was the very lake where my grandmother used to take her blackbird. This came in useful when I had to explain my frequent absences to my mother. Not only had the white blackbird outlived my grandmother, but so had its 'bride,' sold to us by the blind man. My mother ended up accepting—and appreciating—my twice-weekly visits to the bird lake; two times, once per bird, because I argued that the cages were extremely heavy and I could not carry both blackbirds at once. Naturally, nobody kept track in any reliable way, and it was not uncommon for me to go to the park three times a week, not necessarily alternating the cages or the birds.

It was unusual in those days to see a girl on her own in a public park; so unusual in fact that in the beginning, more than one adult (and more than one old person out walking their bird) approached me to ask if I was lost. As soon as they saw the cage, or moreover, saw me engrossed in copying down trees and plants, their initial alarm gave way to a kind of admiration. They found my drawings—my pitiful scribbling—commendable. My decision to keep taking out my grandmother's bird even elicited a few tears from some of the old women who had been with her only a few months before.

Seeing how easily they accepted me at the park fuelled my courage, and like a smuggler, I finally hid one of the heavy books belonging to my grandmother underneath the handy blue cloth (running the risk of harming the bird) so that I could finally make a direct comparison.

It was a very cold afternoon, and there were few people in the park. I can imagine how I must have looked: a fourteen-year-old girl (who looked even younger) sitting on a stone bench with an old bamboo cage by her side and an immense book on her lap, absorbed in reading, looking up only to observe a nearby tree or plant. The image, curiously enough, must have attracted Xiaomei, given the combination of her father's passion for birds and hers for botany. And so, when I least expected it, I looked up from the book and saw the girl whose beauty had drawn me to the park in the first place.

I had it so set in my mind that Xiaomei only went to the park at certain hours of the morning, that seeing her there in the afternoon seemed like an anomaly. In my imagination, I had planned our meeting differently: seeing her standing in front of a tree, I would approach her and tell her the exact name of the specimen. Yet again, what actually happened was unexpected and far more interesting. I was incredibly proud that my presence had aroused her curiosity, but I also felt a mixture of shyness and embarrassment. Before I could react, Xiaomei sat down next to me and looked at the weighty book in my lap.

Is that yours? she asked.

I was about to reply when the blackbird suddenly let out a chirp, and I remembered that it was the one her father had sold us. Xiaomei did not appear to recognise it; nor did she seem to recognise me. At that moment, I was not a customer at the market. I was a girl with a magnificent book. Better that way, I thought.

I had never observed Xiaomei so closely before, and without fear of exaggeration, I can say that for a couple of minutes it seemed like some sort of absurd contest over which of us was more absorbed—Xiaomei looking at the book, or me looking at Xiaomei.

Thanks, I suppose, to the book, she did not notice how flustered I was. Close up, even dressed in her clothes for the market, Xiaomei seemed both unfamiliar and familiar at the same time. It was definitely her, although she seemed dissociated from the Xiaomei lodged in my memory. It was almost the same as with my sketches of trees, I thought. And then there was the fragrance emanating from her hair. I closed my eyes so I could breathe in her scent without distraction, but I realised that by doing so, I was missing out on the spectacle of her face. When I opened my eyes, she was looking at me.

My name is Xiaomei, she said.

I had to restrain myself from saying that I knew, and after that effort, I managed to quietly mumble my name, as if overcome by embarrassment.

Ling? asked Xiaomei. Your name is Ling?

I was about to say 'no' and clarify my real name, but instead I just smiled. I liked the name she had given me; I liked her calling me a different name. She was special to me. I gave her the privilege of renaming me.

That afternoon we talked very little—although we sat on the bench for two hours—and our conversation revolved around my grandmother's book. I did not show her the sheets of paper with my notes and drawings. I did not ask her any questions. She asked me if I came to the park often, and, as we were about to say goodbye (I was the one who said, at some point, that it was getting late and my mother would be worried), she asked if we could meet the following day, there on the same bench at the foot of the two immense willow trees, and if I could bring the book with me again.

Grandmother, she says, Do you see Xiaomei's eyes? Do you see her beauty?

I only see my granddaughter in these dreams, but I pay close attention to her stories and I believe in them.

You only see me? I'm all you see in the world?

She cannot conceal a hint of satisfaction in her voice.

I see out of necessity, I say. We see, first and foremost, what we need to see. Sometimes, I know, your eyes only see Xiaomei. Isn't that the same, in some respects, as what happens to me?

It may seem strange, but at no point did I think that Xiaomei might disappoint me, either because her intelligence or kindness might not be equal to her beauty, or because I might be too immature and my company might bore her. It did not occur to me to consider what we would do during the darkest days of winter when the park would be covered with frost or snow. There were only two ways in which I measured time: the time when I was finally with Xiaomei, or the time when I was counting down the hours until our next meeting. Fortunately, I never had to wait more than three days to be with her again.

I dare not say what effect—if any—our meetings had on Xiaomei. On the other hand, I am well aware that I started to imitate aspects of her without even taking the trouble to hide it. I began by cutting myself a fringe similar to hers, even though it did not really go with my long plaits and even though the shape of my face—narrower from the front—was so different from hers that the look far from flattered me. I moved on to other perhaps less obvious details, like the way she held her pencil when she wrote, or the way she crossed her legs when she sat down.

Xiaomei's individuality lay in the fact that she was poor, yet she dressed with a certain boldness that was worthy of many well-to-do girls; her style was unique because, far from being an imitation, her boldness was original.

Unlike the girls of that era who increasingly opted for tight-fitting clothing, Xiaomei wore a rather loose *qipao* that hid the contours of her tiny figure. She had dared, however, to make a cut in the skirt, a large side slit. She also shortened her sleeves herself, so that her wrists were always visible, showing off the hands I so admired. Xiaomei was so intent on defying convention that one day she cut her hair to just beneath her ear lobes and trimmed her fringe on the diagonal, in a sort of slanting style that covered her right eyebrow more than her left. It was such an unusual look that many adults were perplexed by it; and I think that her father, had he not been blind and not had such a tolerant wife, would have taken action on the matter.

Influenced by Xiaomei, I also made a couple of adjustments to my *qipao* (I shortened the sleeves slightly and made a slit in the skirt) and even more drastically, I asked her to help me do away with my plaits and replace them with a haircut like hers. Amazingly, she not only agreed, but also appeared in the park a week later with a pair of scissors, which she told me she had borrowed from her mother. She made me sit down on the bench and set about lopping off my hair, although without going as far as cutting my fringe on the diagonal. She reserved that particular boldness for herself.

This was nothing short of a pact between the two of us.

The day inevitably came when my mother noticed this series of changes. She made a less than kind remark about me that Li

Juangqing passed on to me shortly afterward. She said that I had become—I can clearly remember the word she used—'stylised.' In those days, my mother occasionally received a fashion magazine published in Shanghai. It was a publication that these days one would call conservative: the clothes and hairstyles in it had gone out of fashion in the West five or six years earlier. My mother could not work out where I was getting the inspiration for my hair and the way I dressed; it was so different from her magazines or anything she usually saw on the street. I, for my part, did not understand the origins of Xiaomei's style of dress. Was it her own invention? Or was she imitating, in turn, a woman she had seen at the market? The country was experiencing a period of change, and every so often, in the tea market or the area around the temple, you would see a man wearing a hat and tie (something unthinkable years earlier) or a waft of Western perfume on a woman.

In one of my mother's magazines, I was surprised to come across a large photograph of Ruan Lingyu. I cut it out, or rather ripped it out without permission (for which I was seriously reprimanded), and I put it up on the wall of my bedroom, above my bed. My mother explained to my father that I had put the photo of Ruan Lingyu there because she had the same haircut as me. She made this remark when all four of us were sitting around the dinner table. I think it was a Friday night. My brother burst out laughing and added that it was actually Ruan Lingyu who had copied me. I let them laugh at me, even poke fun at me, so that my father would not make me take the picture down off my wall. Fortunately, my father examined the photo the next day, as if assessing another potential candidate for his son, and although he pursed his lips and made a face that was hard to read, it did not seem to imply anything irreparable.

The important thing was that nobody knew I had put up that portrait in homage to Xiaomei because I had no photos of her. Even if I had, I would still not have dared to display them like that. I did not want anybody to know that when I was looking at Ruan Lingyu, I was seeing another woman.

Over the years, I learned of many people who, after idolising a picture of a particular actress or actor as a symbol of beauty, one day fell in love with someone who resembled the model: an approximate version, something 'inferior' perhaps, but accessible. In my case, however, the famous actress was the 'substitute version' of my true ideal. Xiaomei was the 'original,' the 'mould,' to such an extent that I was not surprised when, a few months later, she nonchalantly told me she had never even heard of the actress Ruan Lingyu.

We had been meeting in the park for three months. She would often help me carry the cage down to the lake, where the numerous old people who used to gather there, feeding breadcrumbs to the ducks, watched us amiably. On the few occasions when they spoke to us, they treated us as if we were sisters.

Just as I had failed to correct Xiaomei when she called me Ling, we did not correct the old people in their assumption. It was an honour for me: it meant that, in a way, they thought I looked like her. But we rarely went to the lake. Our shared passion was for botany (I always had one of my grandmother's books with me) and when we took a break from botany, we talked about our families. I was the one who asked more questions, partly because I could not control my curiosity and partly because Xiaomei was very talkative. She was always willing to tell me about episodes in her life.

To reach our exact meeting place (the stone bench beneath the great old willow trees), we had to cross a bamboo bridge built across the arm of the vast lake, a narrow arm that connected the lake with a pond of sorts, which was always covered in lotuses. Xiaomei usually arrived first and would be waiting for me on the other side of the bridge. Sometimes I saw her scrutinising my cage almost anxiously, as if trying to guess what surprise was concealed beneath the blue cloth, whether it was a gift of oranges—they were her favourite fruit—or one of my grandmother's books of poems by Li Bai or Xue Tao, or a magazine I had stolen from my mother.

Most of the time, however, Xiaomei would greet me with a shout before I had even reached the bridge.

Hello, Ling! I've got a new game that my father taught me.

Slightly embarrassed, I responded only with gestures, but I was happy because the games that Liu Feihong knew were quite entertaining. I cannot remember the first time that Xiaomei suggested we play 'Touching Autumn.' That was the name, I never understood why, of an ancient game well known in rural areas, which her father had managed to modernise: the blind man's version involved putting into a vase or wicker basket a series of pieces of paper with drawings of all kinds of fruits and vegetables on them. The pieces of paper were carefully folded so that the drawings were hidden. Without looking, you had to pick a piece of paper, unfold it in the palm of one hand, and see if, instead of a cucumber, apple, or lemon, chance had decided to reward you with a melon—a symbol of fertility.

Give me your hand, said Xiaomei, and I did.

Interlacing her fingers with mine, she formed one hand using both our hands and guided it into the basket. We clumsily grabbed the first piece of paper within our reach.

Xiaomei unfolded the paper to reveal a melon.

We will have lots of children, Ling! she said, laughing.

We laughed even more, however, when before we said goodbye, she unfolded all the pieces of paper to reveal the drawings: melons, melons, nothing but melons...

Next time we'll do it properly, she announced.

Soon, 'Touching Autumn' became one of our favourite pastimes. Sometimes we drew fruit and vegetables, and others, we wrote their names with pen and ink, folded up the paper and clasped our hands together to make one hand. All to no avail: we never got the melon again.

We saw in the arrival of spring, playing at 'Touching Autumn.' From time to time, we were captivated by another game, but it was always a fleeting interest. We spent a few weeks playing at visiting the 'Tomb of the Plaits,' since the hair that Xiaomei had cut off for me and wrapped in an old handkerchief had received a very dignified burial at the foot of a neighbouring tree, which was easily recognisable. We spent another few weeks competing to see who was better at drawing the flowers we found in the park (she turned out to be better at drawing), but inevitably we always went back to that game, for there was nothing that amused us more than interlacing our fingers and moving them as one hand.

I soon became aware that we were limited to games that involved little or no movement because of Xiaomei's feet. Her father had bound them when she was a little girl, but only for a year or less—not for as long as my grandmother—before he regretted the decision. That had been enough, however, for the beautiful Xiaomei to be left with fragile feet, like a tree with weak roots. I had finally discovered her only flaw, and it did not surprise me that rather than being a natural trait, it was an acquired one. It was not due to some minor accident (like when my brother chipped his tooth sleepwalking), but something much worse and perhaps even written in destiny: something comparable to a crime.

I believe I mentioned that my grandmother, unbeknownst to my parents and brother, had gone to the trouble of teaching me a secret language. It was called *nu-shu*, and centuries or even just decades before, it had been the secret language of all the women in the area of Jiangyong where part of our family came from. As they were not allowed to write (or to even learn how to write, the men had decided), the women of the region invented some seemingly innocuous symbols that they embroidered, for example, on their handkerchiefs. It masqueraded as decoration, but it formed a subtle system of writing. My grandmother had inherited this knowledge when she was very young, from her grandmother. Before she died, she had decided to pass it on to me. *Nu-shu* was, in a sense, a code that was as diminished as my grandmother's health. Out of ignorance, and to save time, her mother's mother had only passed down half of the existing symbols to her. The same also happened decades later with us, but this did not prevent me from later teaching Xiaomei a basic vocabulary, around eighty or a hundred symbols that we wrote on paper or drew on the sandy ground with the tip of a tree branch, or even simpler still, with our fingers or toes. If a word was missing, we invented it together after discussing what the appropriate symbol might be. I remember that one day we did not have a symbol for the notion of 'meeting' and Xiaomei suggested a kind of horizontal stroke, equivalent to the stone park bench, plus two horizontal lines to represent the willow trees.

Soon after, I noticed a certain detail that I had overlooked and that one might call a flaw: unlike my grandmother and me, Xiaomei wrote poorly. By that, I mean she did not know more than a few official characters, just the names of the fruits for 'Touching Autumn,' and a few birds and flowers.

Nu-shu was an alternative way of writing for me, a kind of hobby; but for Xiaomei it could perhaps become her official language.

Obviously, I tried to conceal the changes that Xiaomei had produced in me, but some signs did not go unnoticed by my mother. When she asked me one afternoon 'out of sheer friendliness,' although it was clearly much more than that, if I had recently been making myself look nice with a 'special boy' in mind, I was able to truthfully answer 'no.' My voice was steady, but I felt midway between relief and panic.

Was my mother spying on me, or had she sent the ever-willing Li Juangqing to follow me when I went out walking with the birdcages? I laughed to myself. Of course not. If my mother had known I was with Xiaomei in that park, she would not have been so concerned. She had asked that question because of my appearance, my mood, and above all, the way I was acting at home. I had become more subdued when my parents were around. Their talk at the dinner table seemed to sound distant, and they referred to subjects that were far from entertaining. My mother misjudged my silence. She deduced that I was in love with the grandson of Mrs Wu: an old friend of my grandmother who went to the park every day to walk her bird, or when it was not too cold, to sit at one of the stone tables where they played Go. My mother had heard that Mrs Wu's grandson, who was a year older than me, always accompanied his grandmother, and the old people at the park absolutely adored him. Of course, she never properly questioned me about this; she just tossed out insinuations and waited for a reaction.

I had never been interested in Go. But as soon as my mother mentioned the boy, who she presumed was the sole reason for my silence, I developed a vague interest in the game and started to skirt around certain areas of the park with an unfounded sense of wrongdoing.

Although my mother gained nothing from her questions and remarks, I wondered, full of self-interest and fear, whether my parents might be considering a union for me with that old woman's grandson. But I later learned that it was all just in my imagination.

I was an inexperienced girl who had never had a relationship (except as a sister) with a boy of my own age. I did not go to school, there were no male cousins on the narrow family horizon (so narrow in fact that there were not many female cousins either), and boys my age were scarce in the neighbouring families we usually visited or whom my parents felt they could treat as equals. I therefore had to content myself with dreaming and imagining things that I felt stirring in my heart, or spying on the few friends my brother had who were, in short, the only real boys I was used to dealing with. Instead of inspiring any attraction, they provoked a strange kind of rejection in me, so much so that I used to make a mental list of everything I disliked about the male sex, based on those boys. I would often revise that list, which I never wrote down on paper due to my numerous perfectionist tendencies, and an infinite sadness seeped beneath my skin. I felt I could, and urgently should, draw up the opposing list, but I could find no flesh and blood examples to draw on, and so I fell into a helplessness that I did not even dare to share with Xiaomei.

I began to feel like I could talk to her about anything. Anything apart from attraction to the opposite sex. I often put this down to an exaggerated sense of decorum that seemed to settle around us, a lack of freedom to express ourselves about affairs of the heart. I suspected that there was no remedy for this, that we would be stuck, the two of us: but I was wrong. As often happened with us, as soon as I decided something, she took me by surprise with one of her thoughts.

I was thinking, she said, that things are badly thought out. It isn't the parents who should choose their daughters' husbands. Their best friends should arrange it. Take us, for example. Nobody knows you like I do, do they? And vice versa.

She said this earnestly, without a trace of drama. The attitude of someone toying with an idea that has just occurred to them. I was proud that she had called us 'best friends.' However, despite my limited knowledge, I knew enough to take what she said with caution.

I should not have been surprised that Xiaomei had such ideas. By then, I knew that her way of thinking was out of the ordinary and her opinions, if not stimulating or provocative, were unusual to say the least.

That day, however, I had the impression that she was trying to suggest something else. I smiled, then asked her abruptly, So where are all these thoughts coming from, all of a sudden?

By way of a reply, Xiaomei pointed out that spring was springing all around us, that the sun was shining in the sky like a brand new idea; as if it were there for the very first time. As if it were there to replace the old sun, which had gone into retirement.

Perhaps that's why, she suggested, a spring-like idea came to me.

I did not answer. I just pursed my lips and frowned in a gesture I used to make in front of the mirror when nobody else was around, and which I had never made in front of her before.

My reaction made her hurriedly add, I assure you, Ling, I don't hide anything from you.

But she had blushed. I chose not to push the matter, and we left the conversation there that day.

I feel obliged to explain to her that I can only appear in the dreams of those who read my old books.

I suggest that we try the following experiment: recommending one of my books to Li Juangqing, to see if she is able to summon me that way.

Alright, Grandmother, we'll do that.

But I say it to her in her dreams, and when she wakes up she has forgotten.

My favourite of Ruan Lingyu's films—of which according to my calculations there are more than twenty but less than thirty—was *Little Toys*. It is also the one I probably watched the most times during those years, indeed in my life, because from a certain point onward I could not bear to look at the face of that famous actress.

Although I have forgotten the details of the storyline, I remember one perfect, rousing scene in which Ye, played by Ruan Lingyu, makes a long speech. I also remember other fragmented moments: the death of her husband, Ye's move to the suburban slums of Shanghai, and the kidnapping of her son in the confusion of the crowd.

Over time, the film has lingered in my memory like a vivid compendium of the years of conflict with Japan. Ruan Lingyu's beauty and the undeniable talent of the director, whose name I cannot remember and have no inclination to look up in a book, perfumed—but did not conceal—the smell of propaganda.

One morning that year, very early, intent on beating the cock's crow, two men on bicycles rode through the streets of our town. As if they belonged to some political party or militant group, they announced at top volume that in the evening, as soon as the sun went down, only to light up another day somewhere else in the world (where perhaps other men on bicycles would be announcing the same thing or something not all that different), there was going to be a free screening in our town of *Little Toys*.

I am not sure which piece of information sounded most unbelievable to me: that the leading actress was Ruan Lingyu, or that the screening would take place in the very park where I used to meet Xiaomei.

It was the first open-air cinema ever to be held in our town, and people were in such a frenzy over it that two screenings had to be scheduled to prevent disorderliness and overcrowding.

My parents refused to go, and moreover, they refused to let my brother go. So, Li Juangqing and I went to the first showing—I was not to go to bed too late—and she seemed disgusted when, on one side of the huge screen that they had rigged up precariously on the branch of a tree, she saw a kind of military tent and an array of flags. I can clearly see now that the screening, although free, was not impartial. In the name of an army they possibly belonged to or might have belonged to once—but which they certainly had no right to allude to—some men, probably posing as soldiers and dressed in slightly shabby, mismatched uniforms, were collecting donations. These were supposedly to cover the cost of the film projection.

Not comprehending their motives, I kept my eyes firmly on the screen. All I could think about was the fact that the actress who looked so like Xiaomei was about to appear in a land where her double reigned.

At some point, as the wait began to grow lengthy, a murmur rose from the crowd, at first behind me and then all around me. I turned to see what everyone was looking at. The blind man Liu Feihong had just appeared, holding his wife's hand and followed several steps behind, possibly demurely, by Xiaomei. People were whispering, even laughing.

Is the blind man coming to watch the movie? asked the woman sitting to the left of Li Juangqing, her words crowned by a repulsive smile full of rotten teeth. Liu Feihong was lucky he could not see it.

If I remember rightly, the woman tried to add another snarky comment, but Li Juangqing stopped her with a gesture. My hands were sweating and a feeling of rage had welled up somewhere between my chest and neck, as if it were about to rush to my mouth and burst out. Despite the apparent incongruity of it, the blind man not only had every right to be there, but his presence was actually praiseworthy. I thought of standing up and shouting out, like in the final scene of *Little Toys,* which I had not yet seen, but I kept this lesson in humility to myself. They would have only mocked me for it, and it would only have led to more looks and sarcastic remarks from the crowd.

Although Xiaomei and her parents were ushered to seats far away from us by one of the uniformed men, if I partially turned my head I could see them. The soldiers—who, real or fake, did not appear very high-ranking—had set out just over twenty rows of chairs. No matter how careful we were, the chair legs sank down into the grass, making impressions between our feet. The film was not scheduled to start at any particular time.

Night had already fallen or was lingering in a distant corner of the sky.

Since the beginning of our friendship, Xiaomei and I had never once shared a public space. Should I stand up? Should I greet her with a nod? A wave?

The noise of the reel spinning in the projector signalled the start of the film. The projector could be both seen and heard, as it was positioned in the middle of the audience. This spoiled one of the most magical dimensions of cinema: that divine, superhuman ray passing over the heads of the audience.

Shortly after the film began, someone—a child, they later claimed—inadvertently nudged the table holding the projector, and *Little Toys* lurched drunkenly sideways like a boat on the waves. There were protests, heads tilted in adjustment, but nobody went to straighten up the images because the organizers were busy collecting money in their makeshift campaign tent. Little by little, amid much huffing and puffing, we resigned ourselves to this display of accidental expressionism, until a member of the audience made his way through the chairs and took it upon himself to remedy the matter.

I was incredibly excited because, even at an angle, I was finally able to admire in motion the actress I had only previously seen in photos in my mother's magazines. I must admit that movement favoured Ruan Lingyu mainly in the scenes where her expression travelled, for a few brief seconds and with magnificent fluidity, from pain to hope, from joy to disappointment.

I was finding it hard to concentrate on the screen, however, knowing that Xiaomei was only a few seats behind me and that nobody in the crowd (the crowd that had greeted her father so unkindly) knew that this park was our secret refuge. The film would vanish, the screen would be taken down, the chairs and flags removed, the campaign tent dismantled, and there would be nothing left. Nothing apart from the imprints left by the chair legs, which the first rain would wash away. Nothing left apart from the willow trees, the lake, and the bamboo bridge. The simple landscape scenery of our own film.

But there was an even greater secret. It was about Xiaomei and Ruan Lingyu. I had never before—and have never since—been able to look at both of them, and now, with a swift glance in the right direction, I could compare them in action.

It was easier for me to see the enormous, illuminated face of the actress than to see the tiny Xiaomei, obscured by the inconvenient outline of the heads of the audience. I was pretending to follow the story closely, and if I looked away then it was only to appreciate the full moon suspended in the cloudless sky. Eventually Li Juangqing noticed me swaying around in my seat and whispered in my ear to ask if I was bored.

I replied with a vehement 'no,' in case she suggested leaving.

I was finding it hard to do the one thing I so desperately wanted to do. One minute, Ruan Lingyu would flood the screen and illuminate the whole park, but Xiaomei would be eclipsed by three heads. The next, although I could make out Xiaomei, the film deprived me of its leading actress, placating me instead with some trivial scene. A few unbearable minutes passed. Finally, close to the denouement of the film, with the famous speech by Ye, or Ruan Lingyu, ('Our toys are all handmade . . . Foreign toys are machine-made in big factories'), the flickering light that seemed to emanate from the actress's face illuminated—like the moon that had been my pretext for not looking at the screen—the face of Xiaomei. In fact, it bathed the whole audience in the same light, but I liked to think that Xiaomei was the only recipient, and that like in a hall of mirrors, the situation slowly reversed itself until it was Xiaomei who was radiating light and Ruan Lingyu who, absorbing it, was glowing.

At our regular meetings, Xiaomei was usually the one who suggested activities, whereas I came up with topics of conversation. I remember telling her once that I had an older brother, but the information did not seem to interest her. Another day I told her a not entirely truthful story about my maternal grandmother, convinced that this would captivate her; but I soon learned that Xiaomei preferred telling to asking, talking to listening, and that, fortunately for our friendship, I was the opposite.

I asked Xiaomei about many subjects; subjects that branched out like the trees that provided us with both an excuse and with shade during our first encounters. But one of the most abundant and recurrent was the subject of Liu Feihong's blindness.

She told me once that her father had not been completely blind from birth. He had been born blind in the right eye, a defect so unusual that in his native town they had not been able to work out if this semi-blindness was a favourable sign or a bad omen. The youngest son of a very large family, Liu Feihong had attracted a great deal of attention because the family had turned his healthy eye into an object of fearful adoration. So much attention, as is often the case, led to misfortune. One afternoon when he was playing in the woods, at an age when many had grown out of playing games, Liu lost his other eye, the left one. The culprit was a tree branch. Xiaomei could not say which kind of tree it was, otherwise we would have looked it up in my grandmother's book, as someone would look for a wrongdoer or criminal in a file. But in truth, it was an accident.

Years later, Liu Feihong would say that his life was divided into two distinct periods, two cities, two families: the time of his childhood in the north, when he was in his infancy; and the current time, of which he did not have one measly image. Despite how much time had passed, Liu Feihong could still recall clear images of his childhood. He had seen pine trees and cypresses blanketed in snow. He had seen glowing red lanterns shaped like dragons or fish at night, amid the sound of banging drums and gongs. He had seen one arm of the endless Yi River freeze over; the river in which, as he told it, there lived a rippling monster that ate *zongzi*. He had climbed the mountain of Xiangshan to a reasonable height and had even explored the claustrophobic caves of Fengxian and Guyang, filled with Buddhist imagery. He had seen a partial eclipse of the sun; he had seen the Big Dipper among other unknown galaxies; and almost every day he had seen, along the sloping path that led to the mountains, a narrow bamboo bridge that was the source of many legends and which people were forced to use when the rains came and caused a certain stream to burst its banks.

Xiaomei loved to imagine that the bamboo bridge was the same as the one in our park. She also told me how, as a child, Liu was terrified of dark stormy days when he was convinced he glimpsed what looked like a woman's silhouette (he could not see very well with his only eye, and even worse if there was no sun). He was sure that she was the old woman responsible for guiding the dead across the bridge to the afterlife.

Ironically, Liu Feihong had reached his own form of afterlife without dying or crossing any bridge. And unlike those who, in reincarnation, forget their previous existence, he still retained (or so he said) the unaltered images of the members of his first family. That branch may have robbed him of his eye, but not of his memories.

Liu Feihong had never seen the face of his only daughter, nor of his current friends or the people who ran the other market stalls. Deprived of this, he had devised an original system, using the fact that his second life was almost entirely independent of his first: he applied the mostly intact repertoire of faces from his childhood to the large repertoire of voices and names of his present moment. He bestowed on a recent friend, for instance, the face of his dear uncle. The merchant who sold wooden toys was assigned the face of a close friend of his father. Perhaps the verbs I have used here are not quite accurate, because Liu Feihong did not make a deliberate choice; he did not choose from a repertoire of faces splayed out before him like a fan. Rather, as Xiaomei explained to me, it was the other way round: a voice or name would immediately evoke a particular face from the past.

When Xiaomei told me this, I wanted to know which face Liu Feihong had chosen for her.

The answer did not come as a surprise to me. Xiaomei was the only person the blind man eventually had to invent an appearance for, because nothing, no image, had sprung forth in the dark cavern of his mind.

Sometimes, when I returned from the park with my eyes full to the brim with Xiaomei, I wondered whether or not I should include my brother in this secret adoration for a girl I could well imagine on his arm, or even more so, in his arms. Did my brother already know that right there in the market there was a pearl, a half-hidden treasure like Xiaomei? If he did not know, how long would it take for somebody (a friend or even he himself) to realise, to divulge the information?

A slightly childish pride kept urging me to get ahead of myself, to be the one to reveal such a huge discovery, but at the last minute, an opposing force kept my lips sealed.

My brother did not deserve to have me ease his path to Xiaomei, not while he continued to be so apathetic, letting my father decide his future for him. That was my reasoning. If I longed for my brother to rebel, above all, it was because I needed him to; but he consented to carrying on with tradition and this made things much harder for me. Being both younger and a woman, I needed him to clear the way for me, otherwise the slightest disobedience on my part would cause a huge commotion.

At times, I interpreted my brother's laziness as a kind of

sensible resignation, or perhaps a passive protest, which appeased my annoyance. In the end, I concluded that there was no way out of it. There was none for my brother and even less so for me. Or in any case, there was no alternative as a son or daughter but to obey. There were of course the usual ways out: illicit romances, which were starting to become more common; or perhaps they had always been common, but were now slightly more public.

Not long before the summer arrived, one of my brother's friends was involved in a scandal that my parents, Li Juangqing, and even I found out about. His parents had arranged for him to marry the daughter of a neighbouring family, when they found out that the future groom had been seeing the older sister of the bride-to-be in secret for over two years. I thought that an illicit romance being discovered or revealed by an anonymous phone call was something that only happened in the movies, but that is exactly what happened: the phone rang and a strange voice, somebody disguising their identity, asked to speak to the groom's father and spilled the secret. According to Li Juangqing, the method was irrelevant: it would have made no difference if the secret had been revealed by letter. Not only was the wedding called off, but the parents of the bride also decided to leave the city a few months later. As for my brother's friend, he ended up marrying a notoriously ugly young woman. My father said that a bride like that was the perfect punishment for him, as well as for the disgraced girl's family who had tried to go against tradition by promising their younger daughter before they had married off their eldest. My mother tried to tell him, in vain, that those traditions belonged in the past, like covering the bride's face on her wedding day with a red veil (a veil not unlike the blue one used to cover the blackbird's cage).

The whole episode opened my father's eyes, and he started keeping a closer watch over my brother. It also opened my eyes. Could my brother's notable absence around the house, which I took for laziness, actually be explained by a secret love affair? I found it hard to see my brother as a man and was incapable of understanding that he might be attractive to the opposite sex. But from that moment on I paid more attention. On a couple of occasions, I noticed a girl about my age gazing at him, and I realised that she was making no attempt whatsoever to conceal it.

Although I never found out whether or not my brother had had an affair like his friend, a love affair that had been broken off by the scandal, at times I was tempted to believe it was the reason why he returned to the bosom of the family. After my brother's friend's wedding celebrations were over (a great many people turned up with the sole purpose of affirming that, yes, the bride was in fact the ugliest woman in the city), my father called me to his study, the same study where almost half a year earlier he had met with Gu Xiaogang. It was so unusual for him to summon me to talk to him on my own that as I walked to meet him (very slowly, as if putting off some terrible news) I tried to imagine the possible reasons why he had called for me. I had barely gone twenty paces before I felt as if the ground had opened up beneath my feet. My wedding, I thought. My father will tell me that he has found me a husband. It made sense that he should do it in the same place he had dealt with an issue of this kind before. The parents of some young man must have asked for my hand after seeing me at the wedding of my brother's friend. Weddings breed weddings, Li Juangqing would often declare, as if talking about some pleasing epidemic.

I barely managed to regain my strength and keep on walking. As my father opened the door and motioned for me to sit down on one of the four ebony chairs, as he uttered his first words (What I'm about to say to you, I have already discussed with your mother and she agrees), I had no doubt in my mind: after rejecting so many hypothetical wives for my brother, my father had delightedly accepted the first concrete candidate for me. He has to marry off his first-born first, doesn't he, I thought. No, that only applied to sisters. Was he just agreeing to please my mother? I could imagine that. I'm not as choosy as you think I am . . . You see? I approve of this young man who wants to marry our daughter. Was that the real reason? Or did my brother have something special about him, something 'superior' to me that led to such paternal pickiness?

My father asked me to look at him. Then, with a trace of embarrassment that I had never seen in him before, he said, As of today you will be carrying out a new and important mission. My father must have seen the bewildered look on my face but carried on regardless. The mission he was entrusting me with—with my mother's full consent—was not getting married, oh no. It was to accompany my brother and keep a careful eye on him.

We can't prevent him from attending certain parties, or going to certain places, or being seen with certain people, I mean that's life, isn't it? It's just that from now on you will be with him, following his every footstep, and if you see anything strange . . .

Here my father paused. I was about to ask what he meant by 'anything strange,' when he explained that it meant preventing my brother from going down the same route as his friend. If that happened, I was supposed to turn him in.

I was so intensely relieved that I was not getting married—not yet, at least—that I could not summon up the courage to tell my father that this so-called 'mission' was an ignominious task. I am not sure whether I would have dared to say it, even under different circumstances. Mostly because, I admit it, I was thrilled that he trusted me. By encouraging me to accompany my brother, when just a few months earlier he would not even let me go out except to take the blackbird for its walk. By trusting my perspective on things, it was as if he were suddenly treating me like a grown-up.

Of course, my father told me that he had presented the situation to my brother from a different angle: I was a social debutante that he needed to guide and look after. This was so irrefutable that it did not surprise me that my brother never suspected a thing. Even during our first outings, when my troubled conscience made me act so awkwardly, he simply thought that I was socially inept. Only later did I suspect what was obvious: that my father might have also entrusted my brother with the same 'mission' of keeping a close eye on me, after noticing my absences. Those late afternoon absences had already come to my mother's attention (Li Juangqing told me that she had let slip to her at one point, Does it really take that long to take a bird for a walk?), but neither of them knew—nobody knew—that Xiaomei was the reason for them.

Grandmother, she says. Are you there?

Of course, I reply.

I can't see you.

If I turn on the light, it will wake you up and I won't be here anymore.

Isn't there any way I can be closer to you? Isn't there some way I can touch you?

I do not reply. I cannot tell her anything…

Grandmother, she says again. Grandmother?

Yes. Sorry, I was sleeping.

How is that possible? Aren't I the only one around here who is allowed to sleep?

I don't know, I manage to reply.

You were sleeping…

Yes.

And what would happen then?

I've no idea. Perhaps I would end up talking to myself.

There's another story, she says. I just remembered it. You used to tell it to me a lot, when I was about nine years old.

I don't remember. How did it go?

Every afternoon, an old man takes a nap. His grandchildren, of which he has dozens, ask him why he does that. He replies, I go to the land of dreams to see our ancestors. While he is asleep, the old man dreams that he is talking to his wisest ancestors. One day, I will pass on these teachings to my descendants. However, time goes by, and the old man does not pass on any teachings. So, one sweltering afternoon, the grandchildren all decide to take a nap as well. As soon as they wake up, they tell their grandfather, We went to the land of dreams to see our ancestors. Full of curiosity, the old man wants to know if there is a message from the sacred ancestors. One of the grandchildren tells him, We arrived in the land of dreams. We saw our ancestors and asked them if it was true that our grandfather came here every afternoon. They told us that they had never seen you. They say they do not know any grandfathers.

For some time, my brother had been receiving invitations from the sons of Mr Zhao, who lived not far from us, in the largest and most luxurious house on our street. They had an immense garden, which was the father's pride and joy. There were so many in the Zhao family that, while my brother claimed there were twelve children, I disagreed with him, convinced there were thirteen or fourteen. Three of Mr Zhao's brothers lived at the house with their respective wives and children, and it was normal to confuse these brothers with cousins. In total, there were about thirty children and young people, and although the garden was three times bigger than the majority of the neighbouring gardens, the population of the house was more than triple the average of the neighbouring families. Add to this the fact that the Zhaos were in the habit of inviting their children's friends round, and it is not surprising that I hated the garden. It was the antithesis of the park where I used to meet Xiaomei.

The Zhaos' house had tiled roofs and was built in a partially Western style. The furniture also demonstrated a giddy combination of the European and the Oriental. In the large, open-plan living room, there was a black upright piano where Mr Zhao's wife, a stylish woman who for some unknown reason scared me, would sit and play Beethoven sonatas. The music immediately made me think about the bamboo bridge; about Xiaomei and me joining hands to touch autumn.

Among the Zhaos, there were two young men who always went around together (two cousins who must have been around sixteen or seventeen years old) and who did nothing but watch me from a distance, without saying a word to me, in what seemed like a strange rotation. While one devoured me with his eyes, the other would look at the floor, and vice versa. Some of the young ladies had a certain charm about them (more than the men, or at least I thought so), and my brother used to exchange words and even smiles and jokes with two female cousins who, unlike the male cousins, were slightly more inclined to be separated from one another.

The multitude in that garden—including guests, there were never less than forty or fifty young people—not only overwhelmed me, but I also saw it as a danger. Whose idea was it for my brother and me to visit the Zhaos' home? And moreover, why? I was certain that my mother was behind it, as she got on fairly well with Mr Zhao's wife and with his brothers' wives. She had obviously angled for us to be invited over, convinced that in their enormous garden, among the various flowers and fruit trees, my brother and I would attract the admiration or interest of a potential spouse. For it was now time.

I was so convinced of this that I saw threats everywhere I looked. My brother seemed immune to these fears, perhaps because he liked the two girl cousins he used to joke around with (I, however, thought that the two boy cousins who used to constantly stare at me were a pair of idiots without a shred of humour). Perhaps it was also because, I can see now, those afternoons in the garden did not involve any sacrifice for him. Whereas for me, every moment spent with the Zhaos meant one less moment spent with Xiaomei.

I came to hate that garden; the garden others dreamed of having. I also came to hate those two girl cousins who with spider-like patience were spinning their webs around my brother. It was their fault, all the Zhaos, that I no longer saw Xiaomei more than once a week; and this was instead of breaking it off completely, thanks to her understanding. Any other person would have been offended, but Xiaomei did not object at all when I told her, without going into detailed explanations, that from now on our meetings would be further apart. I always come here, she replied. When you come, there will be two of us.

Such simplicity was comforting. I thanked her, told her that every afternoon I did not spend at the park was a wasted afternoon, and gave her a friendly kiss on the cheek. It a was kiss I had not planned to give her. One which took us both by surprise, to be honest.

Soon my absences became even more prolonged; two or even three weeks would go by without a visit to the park.

It was Li Juangqing who was taking the blackbirds out for air. Realising that I would not see Xiaomei for a while, I decided to embroider a handkerchief with the phrase 'I miss you' in *nu-shu*, and to go to the park, very early, at dawn, to leave it at the foot of the bench like a letter. This is what I did, much to my mother's astonishment (You're doing embroidery? Well I never!), and in the end I left the handkerchief beneath a willow tree, weighted down by a stone to stop the wind blowing it away.

At that time, the two boy cousins who used to watch me in the Zhaos' garden were doing everything they could to attract my attention. One day I received a letter which, although anonymous, had clearly been written by one of them. I suspected, however, that the letter had been written by both of them, shoulder to shoulder. It was not strictly speaking what you would call a love letter. It was more of a lukewarm approximation of one, so timorous that it bordered on dull, yet it could not even be praised for its subtlety. To cap it all, it was written in ancient Chinese, in an overly formal style.

What could I expect from men, or at least from men of the Zhao clan, when these two young men, who were older and more educated than I (they used to say that about the Zhaos: they were extremely 'well-educated') were not even capable of writing a decent love letter? As an exercise and a challenge, I set about writing a sample letter using the very words that the cousins had misused. In a long column, I arranged the words that stood out the most to me, and next to each one, I wrote the equivalent in modern Chinese. The result was an unintentional dictionary with a left-hand column containing words of only one character and on the right, the equivalent words of two characters. Then I imagined I was a young man in love with Xiaomei and, before I knew it, I had written a couple of sides of paper brimming with intensity and romanticism. Of the words used by the cousins, I used little over half; those I did not use revealed an alarming dim-wittedness. How could anyone consider writing a love letter with words such as 'duty,' 'convenience,' or 'advantage?'

Was that letter to Xiaomei my way of replying to the cousins? It was not an appropriate response, given that they were both completely unaware of her existence (and in fact, it was good that they did not know about her), and that they expected to receive some reaction from me. I could always use shyness as an excuse; I was not that shy, but it was a useful mask to hide behind so that I did not have to talk to them in the garden. Shielded by this, I kept myself away from the cousins and everybody else; I indulged in imaginary conversations with Xiaomei; I drew incredible solace from getting lost in them.

In one corner of the garden there was a bench beneath two leafy trees; a very similar scene to the bench and the two willow trees in the park where I used to meet Xiaomei. One afternoon, completely unaware of what was going on around me, I started thinking about Xiaomei so intently that it suddenly seemed as if she had materialised beneath those two trees, like a ghost I had summoned. The strange apparition only lasted a few seconds, until I blinked firmly, and she was swept away, leaving only the bench and the trees. At that moment, I decided that my brother should meet Xiaomei. I would arrange a meeting that would appear casual to them; my brother would fall in love (it was impossible not to fall in love with her); and as a result, Xiaomei and I would never have to be apart. My brother's mission would become mine too: to be by the side of the most beautiful young woman around.

I am not exactly sure how I finally managed to get my brother to accompany me to the park. I do remember that some of the Zhao family members fell ill for a long time, and Mr Zhao closed the gates of his garden for fear of contagion. I also remember that my brother was devastated. Not only did he have to spend a few days away from there, but also—he learned—the two girl cousins were among those struck down by the illness. All this, of course, helped my plan to go to the park to resonate with him, but it was by no means easy to persuade him.

At first, my brother said that he was not feeling very well. Alarmed, my mother called for the doctor. No doctor had set foot in the house since the death of my grandmother. This time, though, it was different.

There is nothing wrong with your son; he is healthy. My mother sighed with relief when she heard this. I sighed with relief too, and so did my father that evening when she relayed the news to him. My brother insisted that he was feeling weak and was suffering from the same illness as the girl cousins. It made me sad to see him like that. So heartbroken. Mirrored in his face, I could see a reflection of the sadness I felt at being away from Xiaomei.

After spending two or three days cooped up in his room without speaking to us, my brother finally woke up in a better mood and went over to the Zhaos' house to ask for information. The illness had spread to other members of the family. Even Mr Zhao's wife had a fever. The doors would remain closed for a reasonable period. And what about the girl cousins? My brother was very worried about them; his concern was the opposite of my total indifference toward the health of the two boy cousins.

To distract my brother, the imaginative Li Juangqing constantly suggested activities. We spent a whole afternoon playing *jianzi* (my brother was unbelievably skilled with his feet); we spent another afternoon watching various kinds of street theatre, from shadow theatre to a play acted out by monkeys. On another occasion, it might have been the same afternoon as the theatre, we saw the *chui-tang-ren* working his magic with spun sugar. We marvelled at how, with just a few puffs, he made perfect caramel figurines appear from the other end of his straw.

As if the blackbirds were not enough for me, the *chui-tang-ren* presented me with a long bird with little wings. The figurine was something of an inspiration to me: the next day, using the pretext of the birds once again, I went to the park and spent three hours talking to Xiaomei.

Perhaps because of the reprieve imposed by the illness, or perhaps because so many days had passed without seeing her, I ended up telling Xiaomei everything about the Zhaos. I described the vast garden to her, exaggerating the pleasant aspects and those that I did not like. I told her that two girls were interested in my brother, but I said that my brother found them ugly and vulgar.

Without realising, I ended up talking about the two boy cousins and their love letter. It was not the first time that this had happened to me with her: my desire for Xiaomei's attention made me say more than I should have.

I've never received a love letter. It must be wonderful, she said, sounding like a little child. She had a sparkle in her eyes that I had never seen before.

I resisted for a while, for the pure pleasure of seeing her beg, but I knew that I would end up reciting that letter. As much as I regretted it, after that strange rewriting exercise I knew the thing by heart, especially the most ludicrous parts. In fact, I hesitated for a moment and considered reciting my letter instead of the one from the cousins. The letter that I, enraptured, had written for her, thinking only of her, and which I knew from start to finish. Out of fear and shame, I did not do it. I was more excited about sharing the idiocy of the two cousins with Xiaomei; I wanted us to make fun of them together. So I began reciting it like the heroine in a film, a kind of Ruan Lingyu, mocking the obligatory lines. To complete the effect, I drew close to Xiaomei and held her hands in mine. The gesture came off well. I think that Ruan Lingyu would have been quite proud of me. Then something unexpected happened: Xiaomei's eyes were filling with tears. Looking back, I can understand that her reaction was more to my gestures than the contents of the letter. For the end of the letter, I had decided to adopt an even more farcical tone, sure that Xiaomei would fall over laughing. However, as I gripped her hands, my irony disappeared, and her emotions dampened the comedic effect.

It seems obvious to me now that this had startled Xiaomei and me. But at the time, aged fourteen, I did not know (or did not want to understand) what had triggered Xiaomei's emotion. On the contrary, I was offended, disappointed in her. Could she really have been so touched by that dreadful letter? I was frustrated to see such sentimentalism in Xiaomei; for the first time, something about her was not pleasing, or attractive. Of course, my reasoning was wrong, and it was my own fear that had caused the whole misunderstanding. Looking back, I am surprised that I did not ask her about it. What's the matter? Are you crying? Are you alright? Did you really find the letter that moving? Any of these questions would have spared me that disappointment, which it took me a while to get over. Although looking back on it now it is also true that just one of those questions, which I kept to myself, would have opened certain doors. I was not ready to open those doors, and Xiaomei even less so.

The remaining days with the garden still closed were tinged with a mixture of anger and disappointment. While my brother chewed his nails and waited for news about the health of the Zhao family, I was plagued by curious thoughts. One of them was that perhaps the best thing that could happen to my brother was if the illness carried off both girl cousins in its clutches. Yes, I really thought this, convinced that he could therefore treasure an ideal image, a perfect image of both girls, without the inevitable disappointments that come with time.

Those were strange days, I cannot deny it. Just when the Zhaos gave us some respite and I was finally able to go to the park, I got angry with Xiaomei. I got angry in a cowardly way: without her knowing. On top of all this, my brother started saying that he felt unwell again. I realised that he was gripped by an overwhelming fear. Yet after the episode in the park with Xiaomei, if anybody should be feeling afraid, it was me.

The doctor was called back because that night—or the next, I do not remember clearly—my brother suffered a coughing fit that almost suffocated him. Once again, the doctor told us that it was nothing. Nothing physical, but spiritual, he announced casually. This did not put my father at ease. When my grandmother's death seemed inevitable, my father had organised a ceremony with the help of an old monk. This was met with little enthusiasm from my mother. The ceremony, although slightly unusual, had been impressive nonetheless: its purpose was to give more years of life to grandmother. Every person is born with the number of his or her years already decided, but some people believe that you can give away years, as a way of twisting fate and prolonging the life of someone who is dying. My father managed to gather a dozen people together: my mother, my brother and me, plus the selfless Li Juangqing, and five individuals brought along by the monk himself. These people received payment for each year of their own life that they gave away. In the middle of the ceremony, I thought to myself that the mere presence of those men, those five mercenaries, proved the illogical nature of the superstition: if those men were—and they definitely were—professionals at this ritual, they must have already sold over a hundred years of their lives. The fact that they had not died yet was proof of the fraud we were immersed in. Of course, it was not the time or place for me to express such incredulity.

My grandmother died shortly after and my father had to admit, somewhat reluctantly, that the ceremony had been pointless. I wondered where they had ended up, all those years handed over by the ten participants. Giving my grandmother a year of my life did not bother me in the slightest, but it was another thing altogether to feel that I had sacrificed a year of my life in vain and that said year had been squandered or had vanished into the hands of fraudsters. Even worse was something that my mother had let slip, in her eagerness to prevent the ceremony my father was so set on. She had said that often, the dying person, in their despair, did not take a year from each of the people present, but instead snatched all of them from a single person and this was doubly tragic because the afflicted person died anyway at the predetermined time, while the other would never get back that lost decade. What if this is what happened that afternoon? What if my brother had thrown away a large portion of his life, just like that? I daydreamed about these things (things my father was also probably pondering), so that I did not think about Xiaomei. I was trying not to think about how indiscreet I had been when I saw her eyes filled with tears and how perhaps Xiaomei had noticed my annoyance. My disappointment.

Since then, I think that one of the great differences between children and adults is that the latter know how to hide or feign their feelings when they need to. I could not. Or maybe I am being unfair to myself, and it was only in the presence of Xiaomei that I could not.

To cheer my brother up, my father gave him a bicycle. It was three, maybe even four years since my brother had first asked for a bicycle. I felt like the gift arrived late, and worse still, at a bad time: my brother was lovesick (or something along those lines) and my father regressed to try to satisfy my brother's childhood wish.

The greatest proof of how divorced the gift was from reality lay in one detail: the bicycle was too small. My brother smiled sincerely at my father, but he did not ride it right away and explained that he was still feeling slightly weak. If he had done so, my father would have noticed how long his legs were. He could pedal only by hunching over and, in short, the bicycle seemed more suitable for me than for him.

Seeing my brother's childlike joy made me feel slightly bitter. I was convinced I was nothing like him; I told myself that if Xiaomei were ill, no gift—however fabulous it was—would have made me smile.

A few days passed without any news of the Zhaos. One afternoon, Li Juangqing suggested that my brother debut the bicycle in the park, and that I go with him. It was time for Xiaomei and him to meet each other, I thought. So I took out one of the bird-cages, went to his room, praised Li Juangqing's idea, and after an hour of insisting, he and I were heading for the park.

The bicycle was so small that it was uncomfortable for my brother to ride, but it did not occur to him to tell my father so that he could exchange it for a larger one. In a way, en route to the park, the bicycle's fate was sealed. My brother, after happily mounting the bicycle, pedalled hard with very meagre results for less than five minutes, complained because he had to sit hunched over and then moaned when he saw that, even carrying the cage, I was going faster on foot than he was on the bicycle.

Soon the inevitable happened: my brother asked to hold the cage and I rode the bicycle, which seemed to be made for my legs. Now that it had been used, it could not be swapped for another, larger one.

Imitating Xiaomei so closely proved an advantage at this point: I could pedal because, having copied her style of *qipao*, I had cut a side slit in my skirt. I increased the slit by tugging hard at it, and had no difficulty leading my brother to the bench where Xiaomei was to be found. Just before we arrived, I got off the bicycle and walked alongside him. Although there was still a considerable distance between us, and even before we had crossed the bridge, I noticed the confused look on Xiaomei's face. Our meetings had always been just us. Neither she nor I had dared to invite a third party to the park; I had violated our unspoken agreement, and I had done it without warning or consulting her first.

I decided to play down the significance of that encounter,

but I knew it was crucial. Or rather, I wanted it to be. Fate. My brother who had followed me. My feet that had led me almost unthinkingly to the bench. She is my friend; he is my brother. Act naturally and make light of the situation.

We had already crossed the bridge when Xiaomei's eyes started to shine.

Well there's no doubt that he's your brother, she said, raising her voice, a hint of the first smile of the afternoon playing on her lips.

You're not identical, but you look similar. And what's most striking is that you walk the same way.

My brother and I looked at each other. Awkwardly. With a kind of suspicion. With the confusion of someone discovering a resemblance between two facts or things that they presumed were independent of each other.

Xiaomei found it amusing that we not only walked the same, but also in a synchronised way, moving both legs and both arms as if powered by the same spring.

Looking so similar to my brother was not something that made me especially proud. If there was anybody I wanted to look like, it was Xiaomei, and by that point I think even she knew that. But since our last meeting, Xiaomei had cut her hair and done away with her diagonal fringe. It was neither the first nor the last of her transformations; I was resigned to the fact that looking like Xiaomei required me to keep constantly updating myself, and this new change particularly affected me: suddenly I went from looking like Xiaomei to looking like my brother. It was no longer me and her, on one side, and my brother on the other, as

I had imagined. It was my brother and me here, and Xiaomei over there.

Lost in these thoughts, I forgot certain things I knew about Xiaomei and suggested that she could ride the bicycle if she wanted. No, thanks. She said it cordially, although I noticed her reproachful look.

Months before, when we were talking about her father, who assigned faces from the past to the faces of now, I had asked Xiaomei if she had ever wanted to travel to the north, to go to Liu Feihong's town and meet part of his family; to see that other world, the one her father superimposed on the present.

Yes of course, she had replied. I dream of making that journey. Many people whom my father keeps intact in his mind will have died years ago, but I suspect that many of their surviving relatives will let me see their portraits or even their photographs.

So why don't you go?

I'll do it. I don't want to go alone. We'll do it, she corrected herself, as if an idea had just formed in her mind. Will you come with me, Ling?

Right now, Xiaomei, I thought. To the ends of the earth. But I kept silent.

Even if we both end up with blisters on our feet? she said and laughed.

Not that we would walk such a long way, I remarked.

There's no other way, she said. There's no other way.

In response, I began prattling on about various means of transport. It was obvious information, to Xiaomei or anybody else, but she let me finish listing them all (motor vehicles or horse-drawn vehicles, ox-drawn carts, boats, sailboats, bicycles, palanquins, or even rickshaws), and then she told me she was unable to travel any other way than on foot.

It's stronger than me, I can't. I'm paralysed by an irrational fear...

This explained her look of resentment when she refused the bicycle, which on the way to the park had very much become my bicycle, and so I was the one who offered it to her.

Sorry, Xiaomei. I forgot for a moment, I stammered.

What did you forget? My brother chose that moment to interrupt.

Nothing, she said curtly.

My brother did not ask again, but I was sure that Xiaomei was disappointed in me, the same way I had been disappointed with her at our last meeting. I had forgotten her 'phobia'—if that is what you can call her mania for travelling only on foot—and I had, without consulting her, brought my brother along. Now we could not talk in front of him without his bothersome questions.

I was scared that he would question her, when in fact it was the other way round. Her curiosity—which was inferior, usually, to her desire to talk—seemed suddenly awakened. At first I thought, with shameless vanity, that the reason for the questions was because Xiaomei could at last confirm the various things I had told her about my family. How my brother and I got along. What my mother and father were like. What Li Juangqing was like, what our house was like and if we really had a chimney that smoked in the wintertime. If not, then why did Xiaomei ask questions that she mostly knew the answers to? As the minutes passed, I thought I understood that she had another aim: her barrage of questions was an offensive defence, a way to prevent my brother from asking her any questions. Regardless of Xiaomei's intention, the result was not only that my brother stopped asking her questions, but more alarming still, he soon seemed overwhelmed and started giving vague answers, until he sank once more into that state of sorrow from which our walk (or, indeed, the beginning of it) had briefly lifted him.

I could not believe it: my brother had the most attractive girl in the world in front of him, and yet he was bored.

On the way home, I tried in vain to ask him about Xiaomei.

What did you think of my friend?

Nice, he replied.

Isn't she beautiful?

Who? was all he said.

My friend Xiaomei! I burst out.

There was a silence.

I think she's beautiful, I added after a while. I highly doubt that you think she's just 'nice.'

She's nice, he insisted.

Sure, I agreed, but above all she's beautiful, much more beautiful than ... I had started to say it, but I held my tongue.

My stupidity could not have been greater. My brother gritted his teeth, and we did not talk until we arrived back home, except when I asked him to give me back the cage and I gave him the bicycle. I did not want my father to see me with a gift belonging to my brother.

How do I know that I am dreaming about my grandmother and not about an impostor?

How do I know that it's my granddaughter who is dreaming about me, and not somebody pretending to be her?

Sleep was impossible for me that night. What a mistake, I kept repeating to myself. Now my brother knows I have a friend. Now he knows that the park is not just about the blackbirds. What did I get in exchange for that? Nothing, absolutely nothing. He did not even admit that Xiaomei was beautiful. And I could no longer cut my fringe, or any of that, without it looking forced. From then on, he would see the shadow of Xiaomei behind any of my modifications.

In the morning, before making any decisions or drawing any conclusions, I waited to see what my brother would do. As soon as he asked me in a whisper, out of earshot of my parents, if I was planning to go to the park that afternoon, I considered what had happened from a different angle. My brother likes Xiaomei, I thought. He likes her so much that he is saying the opposite. The idea consoled me a little. I would have preferred him to think she was beautiful, but I would have given anything to erase the previous day, to return to the world where Xiaomei was nonexistent to him.

Although I had not planned to go to the park that afternoon, I thought that I should take advantage of the opportunity. My brother, who had recently been keeping me far from Xiaomei, was now driving me toward her. Was he doing so out of personal interest, because he was attracted to my friend? Or was it a benevolent act; had he realised that the afternoons spent at the Zhaos had been a sacrifice for me?

I cannot tell what was more disconcerting for Xiaomei: my consecutive visits or the return of my brother. I am sure she thought that his presence was a one-off occurrence. On top of this, Xiaomei had become accustomed to—or spoiled by—me echoing any minor change in her. She must have noticed that I had not gotten rid of my fringe, although once again she behaved admirably with me, and even with my brother.

Not two minutes had elapsed when, in the first gap in conversation, my brother looked at me and said, I don't know why she calls you Ling.

This unexpected question left me speechless. Especially since in those few minutes Xiaomei had not called me by any name. Had my brother spent the whole night with this question on the tip of his tongue? I supposed I was the one who needed to clear up the confusion, but in fact the question was directed at both of us. Why else had he wanted to meet Xiaomei again, when he could have just asked me the question at home?

What's wrong with that? said Xiaomei, when I said nothing. Isn't Ling your name? she asked me.

My brother laughed.

Of course her name isn't Ling, he said, looking intensely at Xiaomei.

Is this why he wanted to come? To boast that he knew, and

to cruelly undermine me? To get Xiaomei's attention? Or just to get an answer? The latter seemed to interest him more than the former.

As the answer lingered, Xiaomei stood up slowly but determinedly.

If the question is why I call your dear sister Ling, then you'd better ask her, she said through gritted teeth.

The final *her* cracked like a whip. Then she turned her back on us and walked away at a faster pace than usual.

I cannot remember if, before I took off after Xiaomei, I managed to say something to him. Something like: very clever. Or worse: I hate you. Given what I have already said about her feet, catching up with Xiaomei was easy. I chose to walk as slowly as possible so I could intercept her somewhere far from my brother, whom we had left standing next to the stone bench. That way he would not hear our conversation.

Xiaomei! I said and she, doubling her pace, stumbled. Xiaomei! I insisted. Please!

Without stopping, she mumbled that I had no right to pronounce her name until I told her mine. The real one.

But the real one doesn't matter, I tried to make her understand. With us, I'm Ling.

You're crazy, she replied, and I don't understand why your brother had to come along. It was your idea, wasn't it? It was your idea to invite him, I'm sure of it.

I tried in vain to explain myself. I do not know what was harder to explain: the matter of Ling or of my brother's presence.

Although I tried to calm her down, I could not tell her the

truth. I did not tell her that, in my desire to be with her, I had involved my brother. I did not tell her that I was regretting the idea. In the end, I told her my real name but begged her not to stop calling me Ling.

Xiaomei bit her lip and we did not look at each other for a while.

Bye, Ling, she said finally, and my name sounded unnatural. It had become a foreign word.

See you tomorrow? I asked.

Tomorrow? Yes, whenever you want.

Her anger won't last long, I thought.

We'll see each other, she added, under one condition.

Condition? I repeated.

That your brother comes too, she said. And she was gone before I could say anything.

When we arrived home later, Li Juangqing announced that our father wanted to talk to us. I feared the worst. Or rather, what I thought was the worst: forbidding us from going to the park, or, more serious still, that he had arranged a joint wedding for the two of us, just as his friend Gu Xiaogang had done. In fact, he wanted to inform us that there had been two deaths in the Zhao family: the young son of Mr Zhao's younger brother, and one of the girl cousins who were so fond of my brother.

The news floored us. My mother, who joined us after my father's announcement, had tears in her eyes and kept repeating, Two children, two poor children, oh the injustice! My brother, deeply affected by the news, did not even ask which of the cousins had died. Although it was not necessary to ask: my parents did not know. Since the family were still ill and there was still a risk of contagion, the funeral of the two deceased would be held in private, without witnesses. This seemed reasonable, and I was relieved. I could not bear the thought of seeing a couple dozen adults weeping.

And where will the funeral be? said my brother finally. My father talked about a mountain, or rather a hill, where the Zhaos were all laid to rest. He told us that among the many family tombs, beneath two tall trees, and behind a mound of stones, two famous people were buried.

In my mind, I pictured the two trees that stood either side of the bench in the Zhaos' garden.

Two trees? I asked.

My father told us that he knew the hill. He had been there a couple of times as a child, after other members of the Zhao family had died.

They are the trees of a ghost marriage, he explained.

I had vaguely heard about these ghost marriages, or posthumous marriages, which were not an unusual practice. They were alliances between a dead person and a living person, or even between two dead people. If a family lost an unmarried son, it was quite common for the parents to look for another family who had lost a daughter who was also young and unmarried. The parents came to an agreement and celebrated a posthumous wedding with the sole purpose of uniting the families. In this particular case several centuries ago, after celebrating nuptials between a deceased bride and groom, two trees had grown at an unimaginable speed, and their canopies intertwined in a leafy embrace.

For a while, we did not know which of the cousins had died. It made very little difference to me as I was unable to tell them apart; but my brother, knowing them so well, spent days imagining each alternative, mourning for one, rejoicing in the survival of the other, and vice versa. In a way, it was as if he finally had to choose between them. The epidemic, of course, had already made up his mind for him; but the question was whether, if my brother had reached a conclusion (if he decided he preferred—although it sounds awful—one of them to be dead), the pending news would confirm his desires.

I had promised Xiaomei that my brother would come to our next meeting, but I was unable to keep my word. Until he knew the name of the deceased, my brother would not leave the house.

Meanwhile, Xiaomei's interest in him irritated me so much that I even considered not going to the park for a while. Of course I could not do that; I did not have enough willpower, so I resigned myself to the unthinkable situation: there would be three of us, even when my brother was not there. Three, just as my brother and the surviving cousin would still be three after the death of the unidentified cousin. It had always been perfect with just the two of us, so why did this suddenly seem insufficient to Xiaomei?

The changes made me think. I had taken it for granted that my brother would fall in love with Xiaomei, but this had not happened and was even less likely to, as long as we still did not know which of the cousins was alive and which was dead. I had not anticipated the opposite happening: Xiaomei falling in love with, or even being interested in, him. Thinking back on it now, it really was not so far-fetched. If I had found out that Xiaomei had an older brother, would I not have wanted to meet him? Would I not have wanted to find, in him, a male version of my beloved Xiaomei?

That said, if she was yearning for my brother, as I supposed, was it only because he looked so much like me? Such reasoning only showed how vain I was, and yet, far from finding any consolation in it, I felt disappointed. A physical resemblance was a shallow reason to be interested in someone. Yet I had fallen at Xiaomei's feet based purely on her appearance, long before we had exchanged even a few words.

At first, Xiaomei accepted my feeble apologies (my brother had a problem to deal with; my brother was unwell), but as the days passed she grew more impatient. Is he still unwell? Is it serious? she asked me, when his absence started to become prolonged. There was a moment, after two weeks, when Xiaomei began to be suspicious of me. Is your brother really ill? Or did you just decide he shouldn't come any more?

At the same time, my father had to put his foot down firmly to prevent my brother from going to the Zhaos' house to ask for news.

You must not disturb a family in mourning, he argued.

Above all, he was clearly afraid that his son would contract the illness.

Looking back, I am astonished at how my brother meekly complied. Unless he visited the Zhaos without anyone knowing.

We finally received the news by accident, but from a trustworthy source. One afternoon at the market, Li Juangqing and I bumped into one of the Zhao family's domestic servants, a woman the family called Lei Lei. A few minutes of conversation clarified what had happened in the space of months. There had been not two, but four deaths within the Zhao clan: an old man, a young man, a young woman, and a newborn baby. Everything was under control again, according to Lei Lei, but the doctor recommended a few more days of quarantine.

What are the names of the dead? Who are they? I asked her, although I was only interested in the young woman's identity.

Lei Lei had no qualms about telling us the four names.

As soon as I heard the name of the dead cousin, I suggested that we leave (it felt so wrong to have this information and not give it to my brother), but Li Juangqing said that we still had things to buy.

Your brother has waited more than thirty days. What difference does fifteen more minutes make?

I was about to protest when it dawned on me that I did not have the courage to be the bearer of such news.

I promptly came to an agreement with Li Juangqing: we would do the shopping, but only if she broke the terrible news to my brother that afternoon.

We also agreed that I should be there when Li Juangqing talked to him. I wanted to see how he reacted when he heard the name of the dead girl. Of course, the news was tragic and his immediate reaction would be one of sorrow and pain, but I wanted to see the next emotion, as that wave subsided. Out of the two possible deaths, had it been the one he feared most?

As our parents would not leave us in peace that afternoon (it seemed as if they had caught wind of something), Li Juangqing and I came up with a crazy dare: she challenged me to ride the bicycle blindfolded. My brother took the bait and wanted to come with us. Li Juangqing could think up things like that so easily, that I wonder how many excuses she invented to free herself, if only momentarily, from my mother's orders. As if we had already discussed it, Li Juangqing took the bicycle by its leather handlebars and led us away from the house, down a winding road to an area of wasteland I had never dared set foot in before, but which she moved through with absolute confidence. The sun was setting behind a jagged curtain of cypress trees, and the heat was beginning to subside. I waited eagerly for Li Juangqing to give my brother the news on the way there, so he would be inconsolable (I could not imagine any other way) and the challenge would be immediately forgotten. However, Li Juangqing did not say a word. My fear grew. Would I have to cover my eyes and ride blindly over the rocky ground? Oblivious to these thoughts, my brother wanted to know the stakes of the dare. Li Juangqing seemed to hesitate for the first time. In the end, she explained that if I passed the test she would row me out in the boat on the lake where my grandmother used to take her blackbird. If not, I would have to do the rowing. All I could do was give her a sympathetic look. It was also an unpleasant task for Li Juangqing to be the bearer of bad news: a boat trip was not bad, I reflected, as a means of compensation. I presumed she was going to win.

No matter how efficient she was at inventing stories, Li Juangqing had forgotten to bring a cloth or a piece of fabric to blindfold me. We solved this by using a red handkerchief that I happened to have in one of my pockets, and suddenly, I thought I understood how Xiaomei's father felt. Almost total darkness. For some unknown reason, Li Juangqing's voice evoked my mother's face. My brother's voice evoked my father's face. My mother said: If you aren't sure about it, if you think it's too dangerous, we can call off the challenge. My father replied that he hoped he had not walked all that way just to see me chicken out. My mother then replied, albeit in a very sarcastic tone that was unlike her, that if it were a choice between seriously injuring myself and having to row the boat, or just having to row the boat, she would advise the second option. It was my brother's laughter (not my father's, because, of course, he never laughed) that encouraged me to pedal away blindly. My only plan was not falling off, or at least, falling off in the least painful way possible.

The fall came swiftly, but it was slow, even elegant in a way... Or so I thought. I did not see it. The fact is that, after taking off the handkerchief, I saw my brother and Li Juangqing looking at me admiringly, not knowing what to make of it. I had ridden a good few metres, several metres, until I tumbled off. I had ridden fairly well and fallen quite gracefully...

I guess it's Li Juangqing who'll be rowing the boat, said my brother, not teasing, just thinking aloud.

Would he feel the same doubt when Li Juangqing told him the name of the deceased? Like in the challenge we had just completed, it would be very difficult to separate success from defeat.

Glancing sidelong at me, Li Juangqing said that she accepted my victory and that she would row on the lake. Completely unexpectedly, the name of the dead girl just slipped out of my mouth. Perhaps I felt it was unfair that Li Juangqing would have to row as well as deliver the bad news. Perhaps I drew courage from my cycling prowess.

Why did you say that name? asked my brother, his eyes widening.

We met Lei Lei a little while ago. She told us the names of the Zhaos who died.

What was more disconcerting? How easy it was to pedal blindfolded, or how easy it was to say this to my brother?

The bicycle challenge had taken time, and night was almost falling. The dim light prevented me from assessing my brother's reaction. However, I concluded that the surviving cousin was the one he loved more. Why did I cling to that conclusion? Why did I insist on thinking that my brother must have preferred one over the other?

I suppose I needed him to still be in love, so that he would not reciprocate Xiaomei's interest.

I know what we'll do, she says. I'll tell you the stories again that you told me and that you've forgotten. Like the one by Xi Shi.

Xi Shi? I reply.

The famous beauty, Xi Shi, who always seemed sad and was always frowning.

No reaction from me. She can tell that I don't remember the story, so she goes on:

In the same town, there lived a girl who admired her and heard nothing but praise for Xi Shi. Thinking she could be beautiful too if she only imitated her, the girl began to feign the same expression. Her mother told her to stop doing it, but she would not listen. The girl was frowning because she did not understand that Xi Shi was beautiful whether or not she frowned.

This is how events unfolded: there were two more months of quarantine until the Zhaos felt that the epidemic was over. Then they revealed the names of the deceased: they were the four mentioned by Lei Lei. After this, they reopened the enormous garden gates.

It was already spring. The lotuses had bloomed, but the garden was no longer filled with happiness for my brother, nor for me: I was only there with him at the request of my father, and yet again I had to tear myself away from Xiaomei.

It did not take long for me to realise that the surviving cousin was the one he was less enamoured with. Until then, I had confidently supposed that the two young women were interchangeable regardless of whether my brother preferred one or the other; but the absence of one of them proved me wrong. Without the charm draped over her like a cloak of light by the dead cousin, the living cousin looked drab, as if suddenly stripped of all her fabulous makeup. It is not uncommon to see bland women who are attracted to extremes; they cling to others who are much more beautiful or ugly than themselves. The effects of these alliances appear to depend on intangible facts. There are some dull women who take on a strange beauty when in the company of an ugly woman; and then there are some who, inversely, are not disadvantaged by lacking beauty or elegance around them. In the case of the surviving cousin, it was undeniable that loneliness did not agree with her. And what was worse, she made no attempt to conceal the advantages of the death for her. It had undoubtedly paved her way to my brother.

In that sense, they had not stopped being a trio. He spoke to the living one about the dead one; the living cousin lowered her eyes and eulogised between one long sigh and the next even longer sigh. However, on a more concrete level, there were now only two of them. The surviving cousin no longer had her friend-rival, and my brother no longer had an excuse to put off choosing between them.

The unscrupulous nature of the surviving cousin (she was not supposed to show any joy until at least a year had passed since the other's death) was not what bothered my brother the most. The young woman wanted to prevent him from visiting the tomb; a visit he had to make but had been putting off through pain or cowardice, not through lack of love. When she realised that it would be impossible to stop him doing so, the surviving cousin decided to discourage him from going on his own, at least.

The situation worsened when she suggested that, after the 'unfortunate death,' it would be wise for them to get married. She did not say this explicitly of course; but because of his upbringing, my brother would not expect a woman to tell him such things, not even indirectly. It would be even more unacceptable for her to do it in front of his beloved's tomb. Which is exactly what happened.

Unlike my brother, who was at the mercy of just one cousin, when I returned to the Zhao family's garden, I found that my two admirers were still very much alive and that none of the recent events (the illness, the quarantines, the deaths) seemed to have made them grow up in any way.

Little by little, however, I noticed something unexpected about one of them: while one of the cousins smiled or gesticulated at me from a distance, so theatrically that it almost seemed like he was mocking me, the other one actively tried *not* to look at me, or at least not to be caught staring at me. Their behaviour created a paradox: the cousin who wanted to go unnoticed was the one who attracted my attention the most, while the other prompted only rejection. Was this new way of behaving, which defined new fixed roles and made them no longer interchangeable, the result of some arrangement between them? Had they tossed a coin? Had I been the object of some kind of contest, or agreement? This is what I pondered indignantly, convinced that they were completely immature, until my brother and I were summoned once again to my father's study, and the impossible happened: my overjoyed father and my mother announced in unison that they had confirmed two marriage arrangements with the Zhaos. My brother would marry, of course, the surviving girl cousin. I got one of the boy cousins. I paid little attention to his name when my mother told me, perhaps because I had no idea what either of them was called.

I deduced that it must have been the one who was always staring at me. He must have known about it already; and so must the other one, who was always trying not to look at me.

My father was confident that he had sealed the finest of agreements. The Zhaos were one of the city's most prosperous families. My brother could marry the young woman he had been waiting months for, with bated breath (or so my parents thought, being oblivious to the details); and as for me, the young man who was to be my groom was exceedingly well educated, they said. What more could you ask for? Of course, I weighed things up differently and felt a great deal sorrier for my brother than for myself: he was in love with the cousin who had died, while her successor increasingly inspired his rejection. How unfair, I thought, and my heart tightened. He had been so close to getting something short of impossible: an arranged marriage that did not exclude the possibility of love. My case was different. I did not love any other man (living or dead) and felt utter disdain for both cousins.

My brother was so dejected after the wedding announcement that, for a while, I forgot that I too was getting married. Moreover, the next time I saw Xiaomei I told her what had happened to my brother and, completely unpremeditated, I neglected to mention anything about my marriage.

There's no way of going against your father's decision, said Xiaomei. Then she immediately corrected herself. Well, there is one way, and it's what my father did: you could run away.

I knew that Liu Feihong had escaped from his village, but I did not know why.

That afternoon, Xiaomei told me how her father had escaped after finding out that his clan had arranged a wedding with a young woman. He had never seen her face (he was already blind, and he did not know her from before), but he had heard her voice and he found it unbearable.

Up until then, I had not paid enough attention to the sound of Xiaomei's voice and must admit that my devotion to her was almost entirely limited to the visual. That afternoon, however, inspired by her story, I closed my eyes and thought how melodious it was. As well as sounding naturally agreeable, Xiaomei masterfully pronounced each and every one of her words.

The voice was not, I heard her saying, the only thing that caused my father to run away. My mother does not have, I admit, the most beautiful voice in the world, but by then my father was already in love and was set on marrying her, even if it meant going against his family's wishes.

But has your father seen your mother's face? I was curious to know.

He saw it before he went blind. Sometimes he even exaggerates, saying that it was the last face he saw before he lost his second eye. In any case, what my father remembers of my mother is a girl of fifteen or sixteen years of age, like I am now.

The idea that Xiaomei would soon be older than her mother's image was disturbing to me, but I said nothing, because she had started narrating the adventures of the elopement. That is when I discovered that Xiaomei had inherited her fear of having her feet off the ground from Liu Feihong. Her father and mother had therefore travelled on foot.

It took them three and a half months to get here, she told me. They chose this city because the blind man had heard of a healer who could restore people's sight. They walked at night whenever possible so that nobody spotted them. They travelled on narrow hidden paths, which took them longer but would have disoriented anybody who might have been following them. They stopped at impoverished farms to rest and eat; they told the farmers that they were brother and sister and that she was going with him to the city to cure his blindness.

By the time they finally arrived at their destination, having told this to so many people, Liu Feihong was frustrated when he could not actually get his sight back. The healer had died the previous year. His fame, which rightly surpassed him, had travelled to the northern cities. His fame had been to places he had not.

Before they reached the city, almost at the end of their journey, Liu Feihong and his companion had stopped at a farm where an old man lived. The old man carried a shotgun, which it was obvious he would never dare to use. My family went to the city, he explained. They'll be back in a week. The old man was not blind like Liu Feihong, but he could barely see, hear, or walk, and smelled terrible. He had been left there all alone, and as well as being afraid, he did not know how to look after himself. The modest house was dilapidated, with cracked walls and earthen floors. Xiaomei's mother had an ingenious idea: she agreed to cook, look after the old man, tidy the house, and do everything that needed doing until his relatives came back. In return he would give them shelter and food and even let them have some of the animals. Two weeks went by and the old man's family did not return. Twenty days, twenty-five days went by. When they finally had to leave, they left the old man with enough food to last a couple of weeks. In exchange, the man offered them two cages containing birds. Xiaomei's mother wanted to refuse the offer. She was expecting to be given edible animals, poultry, not decorative birds. In the end, Liu Feihong intervened, and they accepted the offer.

It was there on that farm, said Xiaomei, that the idea of selling birds was conceived, and so was I. My father still maintains that the old man wasn't waiting for any relatives at all. Who knows how many people passing through there had been fed the same story?

The day after my talk with Xiaomei, two people visited our home. One of Mr Zhao's brothers, and Mr Zhao himself, whom I had never seen before despite the hours I had spent in his garden or in the drawing room where his wife sat at the piano for hours on end.

There were many rumours circulating about Mr Zhao, which only magnified his air of mystery and prestige. According to Li Juangqing, who came to my room and told me to make myself look nice in case one of the men might require my presence, Mr Zhao's visit was completely unplanned.

By then I had a gained slightly better understanding of the nuts and bolts of the marriage agreement, as Li Juangqing had taken the trouble to ask Lei Lei, the employee who had given us the names of the deceased. The situation was more complicated than it appeared on the surface. The surviving female cousin, who was the daughter of Mr Zhao's brother, had a great deal of influence over her father and had convinced him to arrange her marriage to my brother.

She's obsessed with him and won't let him get away, Li Juangqing told me, relaying Lei Lei's words.

To satisfy his daughter's wishes, Mr Zhao's brother met with my father and they discussed my brother. Then, according to Li Juangqing, as soon as my father had noticed the man's eagerness, he had reacted swiftly and put a price on his request.

My only son will marry your daughter, he said, if at the same time my only daughter can marry one of Mr Zhao's sons.

I have already mentioned how I did not care for either of the cousins, but this does not mean that they had the same value. Through Li Juangqing, I found out that one of them was one of Mr Zhao's nephews, another twig on the less wealthy branch of the family, while the other was the son of the most powerful man in the city. I deduced that the poorer cousin was the one who avoided my gaze, while the rich one must have been the one who made a great song and dance about everything.

My father did not receive an immediate response to his request.

I'll have to talk to my brother, said the father of the surviving female cousin, but he hinted that Zhao, given that he had many sons, might perhaps agree to let one of them marry the daughter of a not-so-wealthy family.

Mr Zhao gave his consent in the end, probably out of respect for his brother who very rarely asked him for favours, unlike the other relatives. But did his unexpected visit to our home mean that he had changed his mind? Did it mean that he wanted to meet not only his daughter-in-law but also her parents? Or did it simply mean that his fondness for his brother also stretched to this almost fatherly gesture?

One thing was clear to me: it should have been my father

visiting the Zhaos, thanking them for their acceptance and making them an offer. Not the other way round, which was the case.

When Li Juangqing came to inform me that my father and the other men had requested my presence, I did not feel as presentable as I should have been. I had dressed and done my hair as she had advised me to, but without much conviction, telling myself that nobody would ask to see me.

As soon as I stepped into the study, I noticed that my father was perspiring behind a mountain of paperwork. They were obviously discussing money. When he saw me standing there, my father immediately reacted as if I had caught him in the middle of some deplorable act. Mr Zhao acted very differently, very naturally, as he was accustomed to discussing business matters in all kinds of places and in the presence of witnesses far more unusual than me. As for the third man, the female cousin's father, I could see immediately that he was hovering on the sidelines.

So this is the young lady whom my son says only wonderful things about... I've come to see for myself, Mr Zhao said, with something close to a smile playing slyly on his lips.

Wonderful? was all I could reply.

My son has been so happy about the news of the marriage, Mr Zhao added, that my wife and I like to joke that it's the first time we've ever seen his teeth.

He paused as if expecting everyone to laugh. His high rank presumably meant he was accustomed to his jokes being well received, even the worst ones.

The word 'wonderful' reverberated in my head. That word did not describe me in any way. It was typical of those cousins to use it so carelessly, but my father was delighted. They only wanted to see me, not my brother. I was so wonderful that, if everything went well and the adviser approved the two weddings without any mitigating circumstances, our family would soon be allied with the Zhao clan. We would become an arm of that clan, just as the lotus pond was joined to the great lake of birds.

Just as he had done with the mass wedding of Gu Xiaogang's daughters, the *suangming xiansheng* analysed the dates of birth of the two couples and strongly advised that there should be two separate marriages: first mine, then my brother's, over two months later. This decreed interval alarmed Mr Zhao as a businessman. Giving away his precious son two months before my father gave away my brother? In those days, nobody broke a promise. The only exceptions I had heard of were certain arranged weddings when the mother still had the future spouse in her womb, and which were annulled if the child was found to have an obvious defect. But something unexpected could always happen: an accident, a death.

Mr Zhao obeyed without protest perhaps because he was as superstitious as my father, or even more so. The adviser's decision was sacred to him.

As for me, as soon as I knew that the wedding was imminent I finally decided to give Xiaomei the news. I do not know what troubled me more: the message I had to give, or my fear that she would not be able to deal with the information. Her tolerance when I had announced my brother's wedding had seemed to me, in short, unworthy of her. How would she react this time? Would she once more suggest that there was no choice but to run away?

I had not seen Xiaomei for such a long time (the longest since we had become friends) that I found it hard to approach her again spontaneously.

One morning I went to the park and saw her walking next to the lake. Instead of immediately greeting her as usual, I moved a little further away, hid behind a tree and observed her movements like a hunter stalking its prey.

I soon had to surrender to the evidence: Xiaomei looked more beautiful than ever. Of all the constant changes that I was used to challenging myself with, to see if I dared to or managed to imitate her at every step, none of them had affected me like the one I was now witnessing, and none had been so dramatic.

Although the modifications seemed unpredictable at first glance, Xiaomei actually followed a consistent plan, shortening her skirt or sleeves more and more, or adjusting her *qipaos* to become gradually tighter. By then, I knew that she had two dresses in total. She had one that I liked slightly more than the other and which also seemed to take the lead over the other, as Xiaomei always tended to make the first cuts or adjustments to it.

This time, perhaps because of the heat, Xiaomei had altered the rhythm of the changes and seemed to have leaped forward a couple of stages. She had boldly cut the sleeves of my preferred *qipao* to reveal elbows I had never seen: slender and pointed, with a touching fragility about them.

I wanted to applaud when I saw her new look, but I restrained myself. I stayed behind the tree and then went home, the shameful taste of cowardice in my mouth.

How long did it take me to tell Xiaomei about my impending marriage? I think it was two or three weeks.

The strangest thing of all was, during that period, which felt like two or three years to me, she seemed to halt the series of transformations. At least that is what I saw by watching her from afar, as I was unable to go and speak to her like before.

Since we met, this was the longest she had gone without introducing any changes. At first I thought that this was because she had never been so beautiful or perhaps because with the masterstroke of exposing her elbows she had reached a kind of goal or peak. Is it possible to keep cutting fabric endlessly?

It makes me ashamed to say it now, but I began to think that Xiaomei knew the recent change looked good on her and before moving on to another stage, she wanted me to see her. She was waiting for me, strangely immovable, like a perfect statue of herself.

Feeling sure of this, I eventually took the initiative. I went looking for her and blurted out clumsily, not knowing what to say, Tomorrow we will run away to the north, to your father's hometown. We will say we're sisters and I'll avoid the wedding.

What wedding? Xiaomei asked.

I tried to explain myself, but it was worse still, because Xiaomei then asked me with a flicker of hopefulness, So has your brother's wedding been cancelled?

I felt more than betrayed; I felt abandoned.

Won't you run away with me? I said in a pleading voice.

Not looking at me, staring at the tips of her shoes, Xiaomei tried to calm me down.

Ling... Ling, she started to say, Suppose one day I made a serious mistake, suppose I was wrong about something, would you try to make me see sense?

Of course I would, I replied.

Ling, Xiaomei continued, I am your friend but I can't run away. I can't leave my father who is just a poor blind man, or leave my mother to take care of him like you would a three-year-old child. Did I tell you that she has to cut his nails for him and wash him every other day, when he does not ask me to do it? If I could marry Mr Zhao's son, or any other heir like him, I would not go around complaining or looking for someone to run away with me. Don't complain so much, Ling. Soon you'll be living in the blue clouds of wealth.

I did not complain. I stayed silent.

If there was anything I wanted to run away from, it was Xiaomei.

I hate you, I told her. I hate you for not understanding anything. Without saying goodbye, I ran home, furious, climbed into bed and sobbed in the darkness.

That night, behind my eyes flooded with tears, I had a dream. It was a bewildering dream filled with apparitions. First, there was my grandmother standing beneath one of the willows where Xiaomei and I used to meet. She said five or six times, We must summon the ghost! We must summon the ghost!

Shortly before she died, while we were spending the afternoon together, my grandmother had predicted that our family would soon be visited by a ghost.

When I woke up, I told myself that the dream must have originated from that conversation, which I had almost forgotten. This was when I was awake, and calm, but in the throes of the dream it was different: my grandmother, still looking healthy and without a patch over her eye, uttered this phrase, and the dead girl cousin immediately appeared.

My tomb is invisible and I do not exist, said the cousin.

I could not explain these words the next day, although they affected me less than the sentence uttered by my grandmother. What struck me was the cousin's appearance. Her flesh had started to decompose, some of her bones were poking through it, and she had worms in her hair, yet she was dressed as a bride, in a beautifully fitting dress. This alone made my dream memorable. There was another scene: I dreamed I was searching for my brother all around the house. My father was not there. Neither was my mother. It was just Li Juangqing and me. He's run away with Xiaomei, said Li Juangqing as if struck by a sudden realisation. It seemed so plausible that I hopped onto the bike and rode off in search of her and him. In search of both of them? Or just my brother? Or just Xiaomei? I do not know. And I knew even less in my dream. In my dream I did remember (as we can remember details in dreams that escape us in everyday life) that Xiaomei was averse to all kinds of transport, so there was no doubt in my mind that they were fleeing on foot. To the north, on the road that does not lead directly to Liu Feihong's village but close to it, I thought as I pedalled. The last scene I remember, just before I woke up: there are two figures in the distance, I try to pedal but I've grown, I am bigger and now I have to draw my knees up. When I do this and manage to move forward, the silhouettes grow larger. I think that my brother is not walking with Xiaomei but with the dead cousin, but I cannot be sure and I am overcome with tiredness and the horizon retreats and once again I hear the cry of, We must summon the ghost!

I woke exhausted after such intense dreams, as if I had indeed been pedalling furiously all night. Worn out, I stayed in bed. At some point my mother told me that she had to go out and that Li Juangqing would be in charge of the household for four or five hours. Minutes later, Li Juangqing showed up in my room, and I saw that she had something to say to me. She'll tell me that she can't find my brother anywhere, I thought, horrified. Just like in the dream, now she'll suggest that my brother has run off with Xiaomei.

That did not happen, of course.

Someone wants to see you.

Someone? I managed to reply, hoping it was Xiaomei, repentant and ready to run away with me. That would show that she and I were united, that she was able to sense when I felt bad.

Li Juangqing said that there was a young man who wanted to talk to me. He was waiting for me in secret, in the place where I had ridden the bicycle blindfolded. So far away? I almost protested. She scooped me up and carried me, with slow, heavy strides. I owe her a boat ride, I suddenly remembered. Then I saw that the young man waiting for me was the shy cousin. The one who, for some time now, had been avoiding my gaze.

Let's go back, I wanted to say. Let's go home right now. It was too late. My first thought was that I would have to hear the laments of the cousin who had not been chosen. Unless this cousin was coming on behalf of the other one. Fiancés were not allowed to be alone with each other until the day of the wedding, and it was common for them to send intermediaries.

Li Juangqing carefully set me down, literally at the feet of the cousin. Then she walked away from us, so we could talk in peace. She went far away, twice as far as necessary. Even so, the cousin started talking in a whisper. I am not sure what was more difficult: standing up or trying to make out what he was whispering. May I sit down? I said at last, and with undeserved abruptness, asked him to speak louder. Far from being offended, he descended into apologies and with remarkable reflexes, whipped off his jacket and spread it out for me to sit on.

On the way, as she walked and carried me, Li Juangqing had explained to me that she would leave us alone but would be keeping an eye on us. If I needed her help, I should make the agreed signal.

The cousin looked at me and announced, I have come to talk about the wedding, we must prevent it. When he said this, I was about to make the signal and ask Li Juangqing to come to my rescue.

I would have made the signal, but the next sentence caught my attention.

That girl is a danger to your brother. I know it. Last night I had the strangest dream.

Curious, I let him continue.

The young man told me his name, which was Fangzhi, and then asked if my brother felt any love for the surviving cousin or if, as he suspected, he still loved the dead cousin as much as he always had, or more.

I was afraid that it was a trap. I was scared that the surviving cousin had sent Fangzhi to try to elicit the truth from me. However, at the same time, I needed to believe the opposite. I needed to believe that the cousins (or at least Fangzhi) were not as stupid and immature as I thought and that at least, perhaps, there was a way to prevent my brother's marriage.

Fangzhi's low opinion of the living cousin shocked me, and even more so, the clear and self-assured way in which he laid out his reasons. I found it hard to believe this was the same person who had written that clumsy love letter just months earlier. Unless it was the other brazen cousin who was solely responsible for that idiotic scheme.

I made the agreed signal to Li Juangqing not because I was bored, but for other reasons: my mother would be back soon, I was starting to get tired and, above all, I had already made Fangzhi promise to come and see us again in a week to carry on our conversation.

I shouldn't say yes, he said, but I will come.

Although I did not think that we could prevent my brother's wedding, the conversation had raised my hopes and I daydreamed about Fangzhi thwarting our impending marriage as well. There was nothing to lose by trying.

When you were alive, I remember, you used to find solutions in your dreams.

That's what I said, I laugh. In fact, I used to lie down in the middle of a crossroads and wake up hours later with things resolved, or at least on the verge of a solution.

And now? she says.

Now you see how problems are not letting me rest. Maybe that is why I come here so often. Maybe I trust my granddaughter to dream about the solution to my problems and I don't want to miss it.

Are you serious?

Who knows, I say.

Before we said goodbye, Fangzhi made one request. He wanted me to ask my brother to describe the tomb of the dead cousin. Tell him to describe the tombstone, he insisted.

Although it was an unusual request, as soon as I was feeling better, I complied. My brother responded with a bitter look, perhaps because I was reopening a wound by asking him. Hours later, however, he reappeared with a drawing of the tomb. It was a sketch that he had done himself, I presume, in the period following her death. The drawing was of a kind of family pantheon: one of those forests of dead people in which the past is reduced down, flattened like a distant object, until there is no difference between ten, a hundred, a thousand years.

I had always thought that my brother had two great virtues, two virtues that are usually present at the same time: great observational powers and an almost perfect memory. Even so, I had trouble believing that he could draw that tomb, having only visited it once and accompanied by the other cousin. This was obvious, and I told him as much.

More than once, he confirmed, without blushing. Wouldn't you have done the same?

Although I found it hard to imagine myself in his place, my immediate thought was that if Xiaomei died, I would take flowers to her tomb every week, at least. Then I thought about my last argument with her. Then I thought about my grandmother, whom we had not honoured for at least a month, perhaps because my parents were so busy organising our weddings.

When I asked my brother if he took flowers every time he visited, he said that it was unwise, because it might give him away.

But, I insisted, you could at least leave a wildflower, a tiny one, on her tombstone, as if the wind had accidentally blown it there.

My brother shook his head. It's a good idea, he said, but she doesn't have a tombstone, of course.

That bitterly uttered 'of course' deepened my already nascent curiosity. At that time, I did not know everything about funeral practices. When my grandmother died, my parents had kept me out of the arrangements for her burial: filling a pillowcase with tea leaves for the deceased, obtaining the paper money to burn along with the incense, hiring monks for the ceremony. My grandmother, being a thorough woman, had left a written series of instructions and had even bought a wooden coffin years earlier. Every summer, my father would take it out of its hiding place to give it another coat of paint.

Not knowing about these practices, I deduced that the lack of a tombstone was a temporary measure and that the cousin would be given one after a certain amount of time, or, even though she was dead, when she reached adult age.

My brother would not let me keep the drawing, and I did not ask him for any more details. I suppose I did not want to expose my ignorance still further (the worst kind of ignorance, about something whose significance or implication I did not recognise). Above all, I suppose I wanted Fangzhi to explain it to me, for it was Fangzhi who had impelled me to have this talk with my brother.

The blackbird that Liu Feihong sold to my mother showed up dead about four days later. I wanted to see some divine significance in it, so I collected the cage containing the surviving blackbird and begged Li Juangqing to accompany me to my grandmother's tomb.

Close to the tombs of my grandmother and the rest of my ancestors, there was a set of tombs belonging to another family. Among them was a fresh tombstone, which Li Juangqing stopped in front of, clearly curious. I went over to see what had caught her attention. Barely moving her lips, she looked like she was unable to read, but this was not it. In fact, she was in shock. On the tombstone, I saw the name of a woman and a couple of dates: birth and death. The last date was recent.

Did you know her? I asked.

She was my great childhood friend, she replied. I loved her, admired her; she was a couple of years older than me and I thought she was so clever and beautiful.

Li Juangqing's eyes misted over, but she made an effort to compose herself.

We had an argument twenty years ago. I never saw her again.

And now I find out, absolutely by chance, that she got married and that she has died.

There's no doubt that she died, but it doesn't say anywhere that she got married.

Li Juangqing shook her head, as if my ignorance was regrettable.

If she had not married, she said, carefully enunciating every syllable, then she would not have a tombstone.

Are you telling me that men and women who don't get married are not entitled to a tombstone?

Women who don't get married, she clarified.

Women? I said. Women aren't, but men are? Why?

Because they are men, she replied, as if that explained everything.

So what?

So ... I don't know, she exclaimed. Why did one bird die and not the other one? Not everything has an explanation. Some things are just like that.

I was not satisfied with her answer, but I was beginning to understand the riddle that Fangzhi had set for me. My brother could not describe the cousin's tombstone, because there was no tombstone, because the cousin had died unmarried, because...

After helping me to burn some paper money in honour of my grandmother, Li Juangqing suggested we take the surviving blackbird to the lake. Her suggestion, I still think, did not have any ulterior motive, but the fact is that the three of us (Li Juangqing, the 'widowed' blackbird, and me) ended up aboard one of the rental boats, and I was the one who had to row.

It goes without saying that just a few steps from the lake were the stone bench and the two willow trees, in whose shade Xiaomei used to sit. It also goes without saying that I did not want Li Juangqing to know anything about this place, or my encounters with Xiaomei.

In recent years, I have realised that my devotion to Xiaomei began to languish (or, rather, to become slightly less unconditional) that afternoon at the lake. As I rowed and rowed, it was as if I was moving farther away from the shore. From her. I am aware of my tendency to dramatise things, but perhaps I was right to see the death of the bird as a sign. The question is, did this sign relate to my grandmother or to Xiaomei?

After a few minutes, seeing that I was starting to get tired, Li Juangqing gestured to me to raise the oars, and I extended them over the sides of the boat, parallel with the surface of the water.

This is the prize, she proclaimed.

The prize? I asked.

The dry slapping of the water against the hull, the silence in the middle of the lake, the boat gently rocking, drunk on inertia. This was what Li Juangqing was referring to, to this kind of prize: a reward for the tenacity of the boatman.

Today I can see the parallel between this idea and her life ethic, which was to work tirelessly for the sake of those oases of calm: the time when it is possible to raise the oars and consider what you have achieved by the sweat of your brow. That is the reward.

My grandmother's old blackbird suddenly burst into song as if to complete the scene. He seemed happy, if birds can feel such emotions.

Li Juangqing also seemed happy or, in any case, willing to abandon her duties for a moment and let herself be looked after, taken out on a boat, and finally, almost honoured by an inexperienced boatwoman like me.

Was Li Juangqing's life made up of these fleeting moments of joy? Did she envy her old friend who, after rising up in society, had managed to marry? Was she horrified to know that in the future, when she was dead, nothing would be left of her in this world, not even a tombstone with her name on it?

I had never paused to think about her in such depth before.

My thoughts drifted to Xiaomei, and I peered at the sunny shore of the lake with the bamboo bridge perched on it like a tiny building. I thought about Fangzhi and his plan to call off my brother's wedding. Then I thought about the other female cousin who, when she died, would have a tombstone with her name on it in block letters. At last I said, Do I have to be grateful that I'm getting married? Should I feel lucky or unfortunate?

Li Juangqing laughed heartily.

You'll ask yourself this question a thousand times in your life and I'm sure that every day the answer will be different.

Yes, but what about now? I wanted to know, impatient to find out about the future.

If I were you, she told me, I would be happy. Marriage is very useful, you know. Mr Zhao is powerful and influential, but his family is not hated like others in a similar position. And, above all, I think that Fangzhi is educated, that he loves you and that he would never hurt you.

Fangzhi? I stammered.

Li Juangqing immediately understood.

What? Did you really think that the other one would be your husband? Really? That's what you thought?

There was still a day to go before Fangzhi's promised visit. I wanted to see him again, as much as, or perhaps more than before, but at the same time I was scared. Our meeting had come to mean something else.

I even started to hope that he would not show up. Before I saw him, I wanted to go to Xiaomei to tell her the news, to tell her, You're right, I have nothing to complain about.

In the end, I did nothing.

I don't want to go, I said, as soon as Li Juangqing came to remind me of the meeting. I was so stubborn about it that Li Juangqing went to see Fangzhi and apologised for me, saying that I was still unwell, that my health had worsened. Nothing serious, she explained hurriedly, because he looked slightly alarmed. Finally, she passed on my gift of a live cricket inside a small wooden tube. My grandmother had told me that my grandfather had given her the same gift when they were young.

According to Li Juangqing, Fangzhi agreed that perhaps it was better that way. Our meetings could only take place in secret, without our parents knowing. In that sense, he added, it was wise not to arrange another meeting. I was slightly disappointed when

I heard this. I cannot deny it, I hoped that my future husband longed to see me so much that he would not mind breaking with convention. That was not what frustrated me most, I must say (since I no longer felt able to see him again so soon, suddenly overcome by shyness), but rather that, according to Li Juangqing, Fangzhi did not mention anything about his plan to thwart my brother's wedding.

I was consoled by the fact that Li Juangqing brought me a gift from Fangzhi, in exchange for my cricket. It was an ink drawing of a bird, which—he told her—was his version of the *dong-zhen*, the bird capable of telling lies from truth. I found it endearing that it had occurred to Fangzhi, like me, to give a gift. I soon realised, however, that we had not had a simultaneous urge to do so. He had decided to return my gesture when Li Juangqing had given him my cricket. Taking out a notebook that he carried in one of his pockets, and opening it on his lap, with a few firm strokes he had created the monstrous outline of the *dong-zhen*. He draws extremely quickly and hardly pays attention to what he's doing, Li Juangqing explained.

It pleased me that my future husband had artistic talent. But of all the objects in existence, why had he chosen to draw a bird? I thought about my grandmother and her blackbird, but in particular about the blind man and Xiaomei, whom I had dared to compare with a mythological bird.

A week later I received, via Li Juangqing, another drawing from Fangzhi: another *dong-zhen* bird. Over the weeks leading up to our wedding day, Fangzhi sent me ten drawings. All of them were devoted to that bird. I had never seen any pictures of the *dong-zhen* before and knew very little about it. I often confused it with the *lu duan* beast, which had identical powers, so I was delighted to receive Fangzhi's version. The bird's most prominent feature was the asymmetry of its wings: one wing had sparse plumage and was long and pointed like a sharp knife; the other had bushy feathers and a plump, rounded outline.

Soon I realised that one wing must have represented lies and the other truth, but I did not know which was which. Was lying like a knife, capable of inflicting damage, or was truth a knife, emerging victorious? Was lying something inflated and about to explode like a balloon? Or was truth round, like the sun?

Over the years, I brought this up. Fangzhi said he did not know the answer and that only the *dong-zhen*, if it existed, could answer. I liked to imagine that he had chosen the *dong-zhen* as a theme of his drawings, whether consciously or not, because he wanted to show me that his affection was real, to set it apart from the other cousin's insincere affection. Later, I noticed that Fangzhi liked nothing more than drawing imaginary objects, things which had familiar names, birds and trees, but which, in his interpretation, did not resemble any tree or any bird ever seen before.

A few days before my grandmother died, I remember the last meaningful conversation I had with her. It was our final talk before the pain, fatigue, and delirium of her illness overcame her.

That afternoon, when we were alone together, my grandmother whispered that she finally felt ready to undertake the journey to the imagined land.

That land was, of course, death. The last in a series of imagined lands; the land we can never stop imagining because we possess no real images of it.

With my wedding to Fangzhi drawing near, I began to understand this idea a little better. But back when I was a child, when my grandmother still lived in the everyday land, life was the great imagined land for me, not death. A life filled with promise of the future, unlike my grandmother's life. A life in which Xiaomei did not exist; or was even imagined. A life in which pleasure and pain were the greatest regions to discover.

It was after I met Xiaomei that I started constantly dreaming about my grandmother; when she started pestering me from her distant land.

At first—I remember it well—I was frustrated at waking

up without any memory of the dream. All I had was the vague impression of being visited by her voice; yet when I awoke, I could not remember a word of what she had said.

The night my grandmother shouted, We must summon the ghost! at the foot of the willow tree, seemed almost like a premonition to me. Was she the ghost who kept appearing? Had she summoned herself? Had she turned into her own ghost? This might have explained why I had not dreamed of her as often since that exceptional night; the night I remembered so clearly.

I will not go into detail regarding the organisation of my wedding. At the time, of course, it caused quite a commotion in our social circle. My mother was obviously more excited than I was about choosing my dress and my trousseau, to which, on her advice, we added chopsticks, fruit, scissors, an umbrella, and even a tiny vase. The euphoria was fleeting, however, because almost immediately something happened that would be talked about not just by our family, but all over that part of the city.

To this day I wonder if what happened was real (although 'real' sounds improper in this context), or if it was all a consequence of a plan devised by Fangzhi, right down to the last detail. There was also another explanation somewhere in the middle, although this has always seemed implausible to me.

The first warning sign did not come from Fangzhi, but from his austere father, Mr Zhao. When he told his family and then mine that for a week the dead female cousin had appeared insistently in his dreams, not just asking, but begging him to cancel my brother's wedding otherwise we would be cursed, the response of the others was far from unanimous, but certainly not indifferent.

Fangzhi immediately said that she had also been visiting him in his dreams for about five nights. I thought this might have been part of the plan: after convincing his father, now he was acting as they had agreed. It was only logical that I found myself joining in. I did not really care how much of the truth they knew. I would have done anything to spare my brother.

Three nights ago, I lied, she visited me in my dreams. She was so frightening... I exaggerated, describing how she was covered in cobwebs, horribly bloodstained, her eyes bulging. I felt justified, knowing that I had dreamed of her at least once: the same night my grandmother had appeared to me, the one occasion when she was not just a voice and I could actually see her.

I did not expect Li Juangqing to say the same thing. I was even more surprised when the wife of Mr Zhao took the initiative and, summoning the father of the living cousin, she argued that the arranged marriage constituted a threat to the peace of the two families.

The ghost my grandmother had prophesied was there. It was among us, and whether it was genuine or invented, either way—as often happens—it was born out of our fears. Primarily it was born out of our fear that my brother would end up condemned to a wedding as unworthy as it was ill-fated.

My grandmother used to say that the frightening thing about ghosts was not their existence, but the fact that some people could see them, while others could not. I was never really intrigued by that. If everybody could see ghosts, would they scare us half as immensely as they do? What always fascinated me was the sharp divide between those who believe in ghosts and those who do not. It seems impossible for there to be any middle ground, as if there is no alternative between being alive or dead... except being a ghost, of course.

The adviser had to be consulted. There was no way, as far as I know, to settle a problem like that except by a person who was prestigious, neutral, and unrelated to the two families. I do wonder, however, if the adviser was telling the truth when he said that the dead cousin had also burst into his dreams, or if he invented this story because Mr Zhao or his cousin had paid him to do so.

The adviser, in any case, had the good judgement not to interfere too much until my wedding was over. I am sure that the intelligent Fangzhi took care of that particular detail, being determined to ensure his wedding before carrying on with the plan.

I have two lasting images in particular of my wedding: the white, red, and green grains of rice pattering on the cloth of the wide umbrella above my head; and the endless bowing I was obliged to do (to the ground, to the sky, to our fathers, to Fangzhi), after covering my face for some time with a red silk veil: the *hong gai tou*. My memory is more precise about what happened after I was married. I remember, late that night as Fangzhi slept, trying in vain to recall a poem by Xue Tao that I had learned, not entirely accurately, from an old book belonging to my grandmother:

The stream, as clear as glass,
Flows like a trail of smoke;
Its strange music drifts to my pillow,
Makes me recall past loves,
Keeps me awake in sorrow.

It was not a strange music that made sleep elude me that night, but rather, the tortuous pillow in the bridal bed. Mr Zhao had been in charge of the *an chuang*, choosing the pillows and mattress, finding a favourable position for the bed, so that no corner of any piece of furniture was pointing directly at it. Mrs Zhao—who by then I no longer found as frightening—had laid the sheets on the bed and the day before the ceremony placed a newborn baby girl (a distant niece) briefly on the sheets. A baby lying on the bed was said to ensure offspring.

A heavy wind rustled the dry leaves that night.

Only the wind can really touch autumn, I remember thinking. Above all I remember the following morning, when I looked in the mirror just after I had woken up, convinced that I would see something new, at best a tiny sign of maturity. The only new thing I saw was my surroundings. The furniture, the curtains, the windows, and the light, all belonging to the Zhao family: this was going to be my entire world.

The bridal chamber allocated to us by Mr Zhao, and which we lived in for the first two years, had a balcony overlooking the extensive garden.

Although the balcony was narrow, I managed to fit a chair on it, and from up there I learned to reconcile myself with the garden full of scents and colours. The garden that, not so long ago, I had detested.

In the afternoons I watched the games that I had played, although reluctantly, only a few months ago. Then without moving from my chair, I watched the sunset. I missed my parents and Li Juangqing, but I did visit them once a week. Every time I saw

Li Juangqing I asked after my grandmother's blackbird; she was now in charge of feeding it and taking it out for walks because Mr Zhao had not agreed to my moving in with the bird of a dead woman in tow. As for my brother, I saw him less often. He had made friends with Fangzhi and it was not uncommon for both of them, plus the other cousin (the one who wrote the terrible love letter), to meet up at Mr Zhao's house to practice calligraphy, read out loud, chat, draw (nobody was as good at drawing as Fangzhi), or even play darts, a game that a dear friend of Mr Zhao had brought from England or somewhere else abroad. I was invited to join but I did not, as I wanted to avoid the other cousin. Despite my marriage to Fangzhi, he had not lost the habit of staring at me with a forwardness that seemed like bitterness; with a bitterness that seemed like an affliction.

You'll want to know how this turns out, said Fangzhi, one night as the sun was sinking out of view.

I gave him a sideways look, not paying him my full attention.

The best part is yet to come, he continued.

Was he referring to our fledgling marriage, or to what I secretly referred to as 'his plan?' I regret that I did not ask him when I should have.

Two or three weeks later, the *suanming xiansheng* made his official announcement. He decreed that my brother's wedding should not go ahead. He decreed a posthumous wedding, which he called *ming-hun*, with the dead girl who kept appearing in numerous dreams.

Mr Zhao and my father obeyed the instructions. The father of the dead cousin voiced his agreement. The father of the living cousin had no choice but to accept it too, for which he immediately earned his daughter's hatred.

The ghost wedding, as everyone called it, was the greatest event to occur in many years. Obviously, both families wanted a private ceremony, but the news travelled throughout the city so fast that Fangzhi thought the living cousin had spread the news out of spite.

Every so often there was a posthumous wedding in our city, but it usually followed the normal format: a young couple who are engaged and one of them dies before the marriage, or two unmarried people who die and their parents decide to unite them so that they are not alone in the afterlife.

My brother's wedding was a rare case, like the one that had occurred some time ago in the neighbouring village of Yu Hang. After the death of the bride, to avoid being married to her remains, the groom had enlisted in the army. After five or six days, they intercepted him and forced him to return home, but the corpse of the bride was so badly decomposed that they had to request the services of an artist to make her up. Some photos of the wedding secretly circulated. There was the dead woman, completely white, propped up against a stand, and there was the groom, holding her hand with a look of terror in his eyes.

Ironically, the only photo I had seen of the Yu Hang wedding—a very blurred and certainly doctored image—had been shown to me by my brother. He had done this partly to brag about being able to access adult material, and partly to scare me. I had certainly been scared. I had not been able to sleep that night, thinking about the dead bride. However, my fear back then was nothing compared to the fear my brother was now feeling. Would they dig up the favourite cousin? Would he have to hold her hand? We turned whiter than the dead bride of Yu Hang even thinking about it.

Are you the one doing it? she asks me.

Doing what?

Making everyone dream about the dead cousin.

I thought you were dreaming about me, I reply.

I'm lying, because I only dreamed about her once. But the others said they did.

And is it true?

Please, Grandmother. Is it you doing it?

What do you think? I ask.

I don't know. I think you would be able to. Then I think it might all be a trick by Fangzhi.

Maybe it is, maybe it isn't. The decision is out of my hands: after all, it's your dream.

My grandmother always used to say, He who talks a lot achieves little.

I thought something similar when the living female cousin announced she would commit suicide if the ghost wedding went ahead. But the night before my brother's wedding, Fangzhi woke up in the early hours of the morning and anxiously told me that he could hear noises coming from the garden. As far as he could make out, there were some shadows moving around next to the big tree.

It's her, I said at once.

Pale, his voice faltering, Fangzhi uttered the name of the dead cousin. I had to explain to him that I thought it was actually the other one, the living cousin, who was in the garden.

I'm afraid she wants us to see her hanging from the tree in the morning.

There was no way of persuading Fangzhi. On the contrary, he was so sure that the moving shadows were the dead cousin returning, that soon I was caught up in his fear as well.

The disagreement between him and me was strange: Fangzhi thought that somebody was trying to return from the shores of the dead, while I thought that somebody was trying to leave the shores of the living. Both hypotheses consisted of a transit from one edge to another, but beyond that, they were very different. If what was happening at the bottom of the garden was in fact a suicide attempt, what on earth were we doing philosophising about ghosts instead of intervening?

Incredible as it may seem, fear prevailed, and Fangzhi and I stayed where we were, holding each other close in our bed. We had not left the bed to have a look, turned on a light, or even dared to speak in anything other than a whisper.

Fear managed to achieve what weeks of marriage had not. Our embrace became more intense, and before I realised it, Fangzhi was panting in my ear and finally fulfilling his marital duty, a duty we had agreed to postpone, on our first night together as man and wife. Our families, of course, knew nothing about that.

I love you, he said. I won't do anything without your consent.

I did not reply that night, the first time. I did not say that I loved him back. It would have been a lie. Yet I knew that I liked him, that he was growing on me.

If I am being precise, Fangzhi did not entirely keep his promise. I never actually gave the 'consent' he mentioned. Of course there was, in fact, a deeper and even more undeniable consent. Our bodies consented. And I was filled with hope because he understood not just the explicit language of my words, but also the language of my flesh. I had never thought it possible to have such an understanding with a man.

Anyone reading these lines will suppose that the first night between us was perfect, if perfection exists. It was not perfect, of course. There was a recurring voice inside me, much deeper inside me than Fangzhi was able to penetrate, a voice that was both mine and someone else's. It told me that he was wrong, that soon there would be two dead cousins and that, as far as I was concerned, I could never forgive myself for not having prevented the suicide.

On the other hand, Fangzhi was quite heavy-handed, and at certain points, this caused me more pain than pleasure. His fumbling was due to his lack of experience, which was the same as mine. As soon as he saw the painful grimaces I could not hide, he withdrew from me abruptly as if awaking from a nightmare, moved to one side and lay there, breathing heavily and staring at the ceiling. I urgently wanted him inside me again. Please, Fangzhi, please. That is all I said. His look moved me. In it, I saw fear, tiredness, anxiety, and insecurity.

I've got an idea, I whispered at last. Give me your hand.

Fangzhi complied. I interlaced all five of my fingers with his, as Xiaomei and I had done to touch autumn, and placed this hand, made of both his and mine, between my thighs.

That's how I like it, I told him.

Like that? he murmured.

Yes, I like that.

I thought about my poor brother. About his ghost marriage. His marriage without flesh; without a woman's body.

My brother was able to get married without any major problems the following day. Although the living cousin was not at the wedding, her absence was not because she had departed to the imagined land, therefore making two dead cousins.

Fangzhi spent the whole day convinced that the shadow in the night had been that of the ghost bride.

The wedding was as astonishing for me as it was for the adults. To prevent an influx of curious onlookers, Mr Zhao had suggested they hold the wedding in the garden of his house. My father agreed, as did the father of the dead cousin. Nobody anticipated around two hundred people gathering at the gates and clamouring to be let in, peeping through the gaps in the imposing redwood fence.

I was in my room and it was early, still several hours before the wedding, when the first shout broke out. From the balcony, I could see part of the street. I was keen to go and have a peek at what was going on. When they saw me peeping over the balcony, the onlookers' shouting grew even louder.

Don't go out, you'll make it worse, Fangzhi told me.

I was about to obey him and come inside, when suddenly

I thought I spotted Xiaomei among the crowd. Was it her? Or somebody else? The terrible idea occurred to me (no, it was more than an idea, it was an impetuous act) to take a couple of steps forward to check. The crowd surged forward, expecting quite logically that I was going to address them, that I would announce the opening of the gates or something similar.

The resulting chaos not only made me lose sight of the person I thought was Xiaomei, but it also annoyed Fangzhi and enraged Mr Zhao. He had been in the garden since dawn dealing with the preparations. He had witnessed my foolish behaviour from down there.

Fangzhi hastily intervened. He came out onto the balcony, grabbed me round the waist, and guided me back into the room.

A couple of hours later, there were twice as many people in the street, and Mr Zhao was quite rightly concerned about how the groom and his family would get in through the only gate without also letting in the onlookers or at least some of them. The parents of the dead cousin had constructed a cut-out figure made from cloth and cardboard. They had been told that the figure needed to be life-size, to represent the bride. The mother could recall the exact size of her daughter when she died but wanted the figure to be slightly taller because if she had not died, then she would have grown a little more.

Nobody apart from Mr and Mrs Zhao knew about this figure. The girl's mother had cut and sewn it in secret to prevent anyone from committing the affront of seeing the bride before being allowed to do so.

When my family finally arrived at the house of Mr Zhao, half a dozen children thronged the street, all carrying their *suonas*, all playing the same wedding tune as the crowd put the robustness of the entry gate to the test. When I say my family, I am referring not just to my brother, my parents, and dear Li Juangqing, but also to the handful of relatives that we only usually saw once a year at weddings or funerals, but who now, because of these weddings, we were seeing for the second time in a short period.

The shouting and banging at the gate was quite frightening, but straight away I remembered that the magpies had sung with the rising sun. This was a good omen, according to my father and my grandmother.

With a solemn gesture, Mr Zhao ordered the doors to be opened immediately, insinuating that the matter was beyond our control. There was no evidence to suggest that the people would enter the garden peacefully. Yet as the great gate opened, the mood calmed, as if by magic. Nobody wanted to be left outside, but as far as I could tell, there was not so much as the smallest scuffle as the crowd moved into the garden, the space provided for the wedding.

Although my attention was focussed on my family—mainly my brother—it took me a long time to make my way through the throng to greet them. Mr Zhao had told Fangzhi and me that as soon as we saw the 'groom's clan,' it was our duty to act as hosts, but all the commotion had disrupted our plans. I lost sight of Fangzhi; strange faces mingled with the faces of my two families, blood and adopted, and although for the moment a miraculous calm reigned, there was tension in the air.

Once I had found my family (but still not Fangzhi), I saw

Xiaomei again in the distance. It was her. No doubt about it. Her look was slightly different (nothing unusual there), but she was as splendid as ever. We greeted each other secretly: exchanging smiles that a third party would find hard to detect. Xiaomei's smile was, I remember, tinged with bitterness.

I wanted to go and get a closer look at her, but I could not do it openly, with everyone watching.

Just as I was resigning myself to the distance between us, the swarm of onlookers, most of whom were certainly visiting the garden for the first time, unexpectedly shifted as if the stunned excitement of getting inside had worn off.

For a few minutes, chaos imposed its random choreography on the garden. Tacitly, without anyone telling them to, the relatives of the bride and groom moved to the front rows closest to the altar, and the crowd seemed to accept that being in the background did not mean exclusion but did reaffirm certain hierarchies.

While all this was going on, I ventured over to where Xiaomei was. I did this casually, as if swept up by the tide of people. She imitated me, I suppose, or was perhaps pushed in my direction because the crowd was in fact moving toward me. We ended up face to face, without really knowing what to say, but understandably nervous and happy about the reunion.

There was no reproach in her voice, her gestures or the first words she said to me. However, I liked to think that she regretted my absence, had missed my visits.

She told me that she had needed to talk to me for about a month or more. She had waited for me in the park, under the willow tree, and at her father's bird stall. At last she had found out, as everybody else had, about the change of plan for my brother's wedding.

The uneasiness I had detected in her smile was now confirmed close up. Naturally, I felt bad for her. But at the same time, the idea crossed my mind that Xiaomei might have been sad because my brother was getting married. Xiaomei's presence in the garden (the garden that so many times, for me, had meant an absence of Xiaomei) was not because she wanted to see me, 'her' Ling, but my brother.

I felt jealous, why deny it? Strangely, that jealousy did me good, as if reviving something inside me that had died.

There was still such a level of complicity between us, that with just a few sentences we managed to say a great deal.

While Xiaomei was talking, I saw Fangzhi emerging from the crowd. Our eyes met, he raised his eyebrows a little and signalled to me that he was about to come and rescue me from the multitude of strangers. Something halted his boldness, however: Mr Zhao stepped in and whispered in his ear. Then my young husband, forgetting all about me, scurried off to comply with whatever the master of the house had told him to do. No doubt, he had to inform the parents of the bride that everything was ready to begin.

Although it was the last thing I wanted to do, I realised I must say goodbye to Xiaomei.

She must have realised too, because her eyes filled with tears.

There was an unbearable silence. Finally she uttered a few words.

I'm getting married, she blurted out, shaking her head as if she was delivering the worst news in the world.

Overwhelmed, I discovered that her father had 'sold' her (that is the word she used) to a merchant from another city, the name of which Xiaomei would not tell me, and that her future husband was a man in his forties who had three daughters Xiaomei's age, if not older.

I was about to offer some words of condolence, some form of consolation, when Li Juangqing appeared and, taking no notice of Xiaomei (whom she did not see, or pretended not to see), took me by the arm, and led me to where my parents stood and where Fangzhi was waiting for the ceremony to begin.

My brother was about to marry a woman who would never grow old. That was the monstrous thing about his wedding. The husband would grow old, but the wife would not. Would something similar happen to the image I would keep of Xiaomei? I had the conviction, it was more than just a hunch, that I would never see her again; that our farewell was final. For some reason she refused to tell me the name of the city where she would live once she was married.

What does the name matter? It is another world, another life. It is the end, my dear Ling…

I thought about our previous conversation. It was completely unfair of me to complain to Xiaomei. My wedding was a paradise compared to what awaited her. To think that in a few weeks, some ignorant brute would possess her treasured beauty!

The world is badly made.

Xiaomei corrected me: The world is not made. That's the way

the world is: something that promises to be made and never takes shape in a definitive way.

The wedding was already beginning. A general murmur started as soon as the parents of the dead cousin appeared with the all-important figure of the bride. I thought about the photo of Ruan Lingyu. I too had adored a kind of cardboard idol, but I had truly adored Xiaomei and still did adore her; the two things had nothing else in common.

In front of all the people, strangers and acquaintances, my brother stared at the ground. He was biting his lips, undoubtedly thinking that this was not the woman he loved, but a blank figurine.

I looked for Xiaomei among the people. She was no longer there, and at that precise moment I felt an overwhelming urge to rush out and find her. To grab that cardboard figure and put it in my place, next to Fangzhi.

Are you alright? Fangzhi whispered, as if sensing my anxiety. I made an ambiguous face. He squeezed my hand firmly.

Of course I was not alright. Filled with dread, I was thinking how Xiaomei's departure represented the death of Ling. Nobody would call me that anymore. The other one, the one who was not Ling (and therefore must have been me), returned the gesture, squeezing her husband's hand firmly in return.

EPILOGUE

The days and weeks went by. I had been married to Fangzhi for a couple of years and still I received no news of Xiaomei. It seems her parents had left after her. At the market, where the bird stall had been replaced by the stall belonging to an old woman who crafted flowers and other objects out of paper, nobody was able to even tell me which region they had moved to. Everyone presumed, as I did, that the new village where her parents lived was the same place Xiaomei was now living. Somebody told me that the 'sale' of Xiaomei (I remember how repulsed I was that they used that word) had been agreed under certain conditions such as, primarily, a sum of money and a house for the wife's parents. My inquiries went no further than that.

Xiaomei had a way of tracking me down, however, so for a while I hoped to get a letter from her. Some nights it took me longer to get to sleep and I would imagine the letter. It was written in our secret language, of course. It was so long and personal that it seemed like part of an intimate diary, torn out or copied out for me. Sometimes, depending on my mood, I liked to imagine that in addition to the paper, the envelope included a lock of hair.

I suppose I let my imagination soar with regard to the form of the letter, because I could not imagine its content. Or did not dare to.

At a certain point, I came to wonder if Xiaomei's silence was due to the fact that she did not want to send me a letter full of loneliness and sorrow. Yet by sparing me bad news, she was only compelling me to fabricate worse. For example, was she even alive?

As my hope of receiving that letter dwindled (although, I have to admit, I never fully lost hope), my desire to write to her increased. Perhaps I could burn my letter and have faith that the words would rise up with the smoke and reach her somehow, like the messages my grandmother sent, as a widow, to my grandfather.

The moment I decided to write the letter, I knew that I would not have the courage to burn it, and I knew two other things as well: that it would be a very long letter, longer than I originally thought, and that I would not write it all in one go. I did not have the energy or the discipline for that.

I miss you, I wrote on the first day, among many other things.

It worries me, not knowing if you are alright, I wrote on the second day, among many other things.

I cannot forgive myself for not talking to Fangzhi about it, I wrote after a few days.

I truly did not forgive myself for not asking my husband to help, not asking for his advice, not exhausting all the options for saving Xiaomei from the marriage her parents had arranged.

Today I woke up and realised what I did not do, and what I should have done. I wrote this some days later, as the letter started to take on the form of a confession, a long conversation with her—with her and her absence, in truth—but I was the only one talking.

I should have asked Fangzhi to take you on. As my servant, or somebody's servant—any of the Zhao family. Even as a concubine. I know that Fangzhi does not agree with the latter, because I've spoken to him about it. Like his parents, he does not believe in concubines. He thinks that having one woman is correct and sufficient. One woman at a time, in any case. He shares our thoughts on the matter. But something tells me that perhaps he would have given in, if I had explained your situation. A fake concubine: a social tactic, and a way to save you. Or a real concubine, you never know. For your sake, I think I'd be willing to do anything. No, what am I saying? I just reread all this and I'm ashamed. For your sake, Xiaomei, I'm willing to do anything, even give you my place in the Zhao clan, or my place in bed next to Fangzhi, even if I am the one who is relegated, the one who has to be taken in out of pity. Could you imagine something like that? But I was neither thoughtful nor altruistic enough to say this to my husband.

I wrote this and then stopped. My hand was trembling as if a path made of words had led me to some horrifying place. My eyes filled with tears. Had I really been too thoughtless to make that suggestion to Fangzhi? Or had I in fact not been up to the task? Did I neglect to do so out of selfishness, cowardice, or meanness?

Until then, I believed that my grandmother had not appeared in my dreams since the day of my wedding because she was satisfied and had no need to. Similar to the way in which, after the *ming-hun*, the nightly visits of the dead cousin had ceased. Now I supposed, fearfully, that my grandmother might not be appearing anymore because she was ashamed. Disappointed in me.

My memory jumped to one afternoon in the park. It was a time when I felt such affection for Xiaomei that the words of admiration naturally gushed out of me.

When you look at me that way, when I've got your attention, I feel like the most important man in the world, Fangzhi said to me one night, after a year and a half of marriage.

I repeated what Xiaomei had said to me that afternoon in the park, after she had listened to me sing her praises, albeit not very eloquently.

It went something like this:

The other side to your devotion, what scares me the most, is that sooner or later you will discover one of my imperfections. I have many of them—some serious, some not—and they are obvious to me. First, you will feel self-contempt for not having noticed what is so noticeable. But later, as is usually the case, you might accuse me, silently or shouting, of hiding my flaws when in fact you were not willing to even consider them.

When Xiaomei dismissed my admiration like that, I shot her a furious look, abruptly turned from her and walked away. I had made a decision: to find one of her 'many imperfections' as soon as I could, and to build upon it as if it were foundations; a sturdy altar. I would do that, and something similar the other way: I would tell her all my imperfections, urge her to choose one of them and to doggedly cling to it.

When I remembered this, my hand immediately stopped shaking.

I smiled an ironic, bitter smile to myself.

I had not done that, of course. I had not found Xiaomei's prominent imperfections. I had not even found, I realised, the desire to track them down. Above all, I would not have been brave enough to reveal my own flaws.

I returned to writing the letter, which was starting to look like it would never end. I looked back on what I had just narrated for Xiaomei and told her that she had now seen my most dishonourable side. What I had failed to do to save her from her wedding was sadder and more obvious than any vain list of supposed imperfections.

Perhaps Xiaomei would carry on with her life as normally—or as abnormally—as before. Perhaps she would even be happy. This did not change the essence of the grief, or rather, the horror I felt at the way I had behaved.

I justified my cowardly, passive behaviour by telling myself that Fangzhi would never have agreed to intervene, but that, in fact, any request from me would have aroused suspicion or contempt.

It was unfair to my husband for me to lay my faults and my responsibilities on him like that.

I had not finished writing to Xiaomei when one night, after much beating around the bush, Fangzhi made a remark that could not have been a coincidence and proved that he had read the letter.

My immediate reaction was anger. I did not say a word to him for a whole day and part of the following day. For a week I was cold toward him. At the same time, I also felt the burning desire to keep writing to Xiaomei suddenly cool.

We talked about the matter again ten or twelve days later. I did not initiate the discussion.

I'm not saying this because I want your forgiveness, Fangzhi said, but I think you did everything possible to make me read the letter. I even started to think that you were testing me in some way.

I must have given him a damning look because Fangzhi suddenly knelt down in front of me like an actor in a melodrama and pushed his face into my lap so that his nose fit perfectly in between my thighs. In that bizarre position, with his voice half muffled, he said that I was right, that if I had asked him to save Xiaomei he would not have dared to lift a finger, he would not have known what to do or how to interpret my wish.

I'm so sorry. I'm sorry. It's better that I tell you the truth.

The truth was that Fangzhi and I seemed united by this. In truth, Fangzhi was not so wrong: I had not deliberately left the letter on show, but I had not made any effort to hide it. And then there was my writing: after a few pages in the secret language I had switched to normal characters because, as I had discovered, my lack of fluency in *nu-shu* had interrupted my train of thought, my feelings. In that case, when I changed my writing, perhaps I had also changed the letter's intended recipient.

Just as I had once written a letter to Xiaomei, which on the face of it was addressed to Fangzhi and the other cousin, had I done the reverse on this occasion, at least with certain parts of it?

We won't speak of this again, announced Fangzhi before withdrawing his face from between my thighs. His expression was unusually serious. When I tried to say something, he put a finger to my lips. I just sat there, feeling the way my thighs gradually grew cooler.

We won't talk about it again. But one day, if you want to, you can tell me all about her. You loved her a lot, didn't you?

I shook my head, upset that he had asked the question in the past tense.

I love her, I did not say.

Instead, I said that, yes, perhaps one day I could tell him all about it, that I would put it in writing.

I cannot wait to read it, said Fangzhi. And we never spoke of Xiaomei again.

I don't know what you're waiting for, to get married, I tell her.

What are you saying, Grandmother? I can't get married again.

Of course you can, I say. What are you waiting for? Of course you can.

The practice of *ming-hun* was so unusual that not everybody could agree on its laws and finer details. For example, could my brother remarry, or did he have to live his entire life in the shadow of the dead woman? The Zhaos thought that he could not remarry, and I had assumed the same thing. But my parents thought that five years on from the ghost wedding, my brother could remarry if he wanted.

When we celebrated our fourth wedding anniversary, Fangzhi gave me a gramophone so I could listen to popular singers of the time such as Gong Qiuxia. I soon received complaints for playing the music too loud late at night. People even gossiped that Fangzhi and I were not conceiving any children—they did not expect, by the way, anything more meaningful of me than that—because we were spending all our nights in front of that 'machine.'

It had been a year or so since my brother had stopped coming to see the Zhaos once or twice a month, as he used to do at one point. At first, nobody explained why he had suddenly stopped visiting. Li Juangqing soon told me that my parents had decided that my brother should remarry, and that this had outraged the parents of the cardboard wife. To tell the truth, they were outraged, but mostly terrified that she would come back to haunt their dreams again.

What Li Juangqing told me was confirmed by Mrs Zhao wanting me to mediate between my parents and the parents of my brother's wife. She did not raise the issue with me, but I heard a rumour, and Fangzhi confirmed it. He had told his mother that they should not put me in such an awkward position and that he would therefore talk to my parents.

I never knew what took place during that conversation, which I have always imagined was between men only, in my father's study, like an unintentional imitation of the conversation between my father and his friend Gu Xiaogang years earlier. In short, Fangzhi ended up convinced that my brother needed to remarry. That was no life for him. So Fangzhi wasted no time communicating this to the Zhao clan.

Nobody expected the Zhao family to attend my brother's second wedding, which was punctually announced as soon as the five years had passed. The chosen bride turned out to be the youngest granddaughter of Mrs Wu herself, who had been a dear friend of my grandmother. Believe it or not, the old woman was still alive (she was nearly a hundred years old), was still playing Go and winning, and apparently, on occasions, even accompanied her grandson to the park; the very grandson my mother thought I had been in love with.

Going on Li Juangqing's stories alone—and inevitably I must, when it comes to that period of my life—my family were apparently not sure what to do with the cardboard figure of the dead bride, now that preparations were being finalised to welcome a living bride into the family. Although my mother had folded it away with the utmost care after the wedding, and although my brother had stored it in his cupboard, the figure had been damaged and scratched over time. Apparently, during the interview in his study, my father had begged Fangzhi to take the cardboard figure. He had inevitably objected, saying it was a terrible idea. Returning it might offend the Zhaos. It would be better, perhaps, to bury her in our family pavilion, not far from my grandmother's tomb.

I do not know what they did with it in the end, and something tells me that neither Fangzhi nor the other Zhaos dared to ask. The fact is, a week before my brother's second marriage, Li Juangqing had a snoop around the cupboard and did not find any sign of the cardboard bride, save for a few paper flower petals.

It was with great regret that I decided not to attend my brother's wedding. This was solely to appease the Zhaos, especially the elders. Attending would have created serious problems for Fangzhi, who had faced enough with his family by accepting this second marriage.

I told my family that I was not feeling very well, being in the seventh month of my pregnancy.

Of course, said my mother. See how you feel on the actual day of the wedding.

But she and I both knew that this was not the real reason.

That day, Fangzhi unexpectedly told me and the whole Zhao clan that he had to make a five-day trip to Peking. I was not pleased by the news. Couldn't it wait until after the birth?

I'm sorry, Fangzhi told me. I know you're a little upset, but when I get back you'll understand a bit better.

On the day of my brother's wedding I woke before dawn with cramps in my legs and could not fall back to sleep. I am not exaggerating when I say that I felt the worst I had ever felt during my whole pregnancy. It was so bad that Mrs Zhao—who definitely held the reins of the household, more than her husband—called for a doctor.

It's likely that the baby will arrive early, said an old friend of the family who had been actively involved in Fangzhi's birth.

Early? I said in alarm.

Before he answered, the doctor stroked his wispy beard and cast a sidelong glance at Mrs Zhao.

Fangzhi was born a month early, wasn't he?

Mrs Zhao nodded and came over to the bed where I lay, unable to get up. She placed a hand on my belly.

Yes, a month, she replied. Just like Fangzhi's father.

The doctor left and we both remained silent for a couple of hours. She was engrossed in her sewing and I lay there with my eyes half closed, imagining from time to time, when the pain subsided, the wedding ceremony in the half-shaded courtyard of my parents' house. It was a sunny day, fortunately. I inquired, and the doctor informed me that there was a pleasant breeze and it was not too hot outside.

Two days later, when I was feeling better, Li Juangqing visited me and told me a few details about the marriage. She had intended to give me a general description of the day's events, but early on in the conversation she casually remarked that she thought she had seen Fangzhi among the guests. This information plunged me into such confusion that I could no longer pay attention to what she was saying.

Fangzhi is away travelling, I told her. He's in Peking. Do you *think* you saw him or are you not sure whether it was him? Visibly uncomfortable, Li Juangqing said that she was not sure. Although she thought she had seen him, perhaps she had been mistaken. Fangzhi returned the following day, and as soon as we were on our own, the first thing I did was tell him about Li Juangqing's remark.

It's true, he admitted, with the calmness I would have expected of him if it had been untrue. I planned to tell you everything and I would be doing so now if she hadn't spotted me, despite my hat and fake beard.

Without giving me time to react, Fangzhi showed me a wide-brimmed hat, a ridiculous false beard and, most importantly, a notebook containing various sketches of the wedding.

I invented the trip to throw my family off the scent. As far as I can tell, they don't suspect a thing, he explained to me in a low voice. I didn't tell you the truth so I could surprise you, and above all, so as not to make you an accomplice. Here, look at my drawings. This is the courtyard shortly before the arrival of the bride and groom.

In some way, I believe that it was another ghost wedding. Even though I had not been there, I was experiencing every detail of it through Fangzhi's hard work and kindness. It was as if I was reading a story from a distant country, an imagined land. I felt as if I had really been there.

Was my brother happy?

Happier than at the first wedding, Fangzhi replied.

That's not hard, I said, unable to resist. He chuckled.

And what about the bride? I asked. Why won't you tell me about her?

She's pretty, he said with a smile. I had the feeling that she was more than just pretty, and that even in Fangzhi's drawings he had made an effort to play down the impact she had had on him.

I did not want to reach the end of that notebook of Fangzhi's drawings, which he let rest on my belly from time to time. I saw the pages turning, knowing that the end was coming. One sketch showed my parents, with their rustic elegance. Another drawing depicted the parents of the bride. It was admirable that Fangzhi could evoke it all so precisely given that, as I suspected, and he told me, he had not done those sketches with the people present, so as not to draw attention to himself. He had done the drawings during the final stage of the nonexistent trip to Peking. He had spent almost three whole days completing them at the house of an old friend, his only accomplice.

Suddenly, on the last page of the notebook, just as Fangzhi did not seem to have much more to add, I saw a drawing of my grandmother. I was so clearly taken aback that Fangzhi noticed at once.

What about her?

Your grandmother, he replied. I thought you told me she was dead?

I nodded and Fangzhi went on, Well, she looked very much alive to me, although I did notice that she always stayed on the sidelines of the action…As did I, of course, although she knows how to play the ghost much better than I do, because she appeared and disappeared in the blink of an eye. You should have seen it. At least this way, Li Juangqing won't spot you.

Did you speak to her? I asked. Did she speak to you? What was she doing there among all those people?

She was the one who approached me, explained Fangzhi. I would never have recognised her. But she said she knew who I was and begged me to give you this from her.

It was an old, plain-looking shawl. I did not recall ever seeing her wearing it.

For quite some time I had no idea what the gift was supposed to mean, until I studied it more closely and saw that it was embroidered, and that the embroidered characters were a message in *nu-shu*. It read:

It is a girl. I am sure of it. You must name her Xiaomei.

A few years came and went, as did the Japanese occupation. It arrived late to our city and was brief. I watched it all from the balcony, just as I used to watch the children's games. One day, making the most of the fact that my daughter liked to spend the afternoons playing with her tireless paternal grandfather, or with her nursemaid (Lei Lei's youngest daughter), Fangzhi took me to the first and only cinema in the city, which had opened its doors a few months earlier. The opening had been the biggest event in years, perhaps since the ghost wedding. I had told Fangzhi that I would like to see the cinema, which was apparently a small and unrefined imitation of the Cathay cinema in Shanghai, with its art deco facade in red and white bricks.

The film showing that evening, the melodramatic *The Goddess*, was just over a decade old (it seemed normal to me that time occasionally seemed to stand still after a period of war) and it starred Ruan Lingyu, who had committed suicide in the meantime, in 1935. It was strange to see the effect of her tragic death: every time there was a close-up of her, there came a wave of disillusioned sighs from the audience. Desire and admiration had given way to sorrow, anger, and fear. If a woman that beautiful, famous, and talented could commit suicide, what hope was there for the rest of us?

I have to say, I felt the same way as everyone else, and for a long stretch of the film, the living image of the dead actress reminded me of the cardboard bride more than of my beloved Xiaomei. Little by little, however, the power of the images, the thrill of the action (the prostitute who attempts, at all costs, to give her little boy, Shuiping, an education), and the striking charisma of Ruan Lingyu made me forget everything else.

A couple of times, Fangzhi leaned in to whisper a remark in my ear, but I gestured to him that I would rather not talk until the film was over, and fortunately he accepted.

When the lights went up, I was only interested in one thing: finding out if Fangzhi thought Ruan Lingyu was beautiful.

My question must have seemed odd to him because instead of answering me straightaway, he looked into my eyes for a few seconds, trying to work out what answer I was hoping for.

I waited a long time, and suddenly I felt like I was back at my parents' dining table, on one of those nights so long ago when I waited in vain for my mother or Li Juangqing to mention even the slightest fleck of praise for the blind man's daughter.

If I tell you that she is very beautiful, you won't get jealous, will you? said Fangzhi timidly.

I shook my head.

Fangzhi frowned and forced a sarcastic smile.

Please, I practically begged him. I'm not going to be jealous, I promise. I just want the truth.

As my husband blushed slightly and prepared to give me his verdict, I decided that if his answer was 'yes', from that moment I would ask him to call me Ling whenever we were on our own.

EDUARDO BERTI was born in Buenos Aires in 1964. He was admitted as a member of the prestigious and influential Oulipo in 2014, becoming the group's first Latin American writer. His first work of fiction, *Los pájaros*, was praised by critics and won a Grant Award from *Cultura Magazine*. This was followed by two major novels: *Agua* and *La mujer de Wakefield*, a feminist twist on Nathaniel Hawthorne's *Wakefield*. *La mujer de Wakefield* was selected for the Rómulo Gallegos Prize in Venezuela and short-listed for the prestigious Prix Fémina for Best Foreign Book in France. In 1998, Berti moved to Paris, where he worked as a cultural journalist, media correspondent, and scriptwriter, in addition to teaching courses in writing. In 2002, he published *La vida imposible*, whose translation into French received the Libralire-Fernando Aguirre Prize. Two years later, he published *Todos los Funes*, for which he won the esteemed Premio Herralde. In recent years, Berti has continued his original work while translating authors such as Nathaniel Hawthorne, Gustave Flaubert, and Elizabeth Bowen into Spanish. In 2011, he won the Emecé Prize and the Las Américas Prize for *The Imagined Land*. He currently lives in Bordeaux.

CHARLOTTE COOMBE is a British translator working from French and Spanish into English. After a decade translating commercial texts in gastronomy, the arts, travel, lifestyle, fashion, and advertising, her love of literature drew her to literary translation. She has translated authors such as Edgardo Nuñez Caballero, Rosa María Roffiel, and Santiago Roncagliolo for the online publication *Palabras Errantes*, and her translation of Abnousse Shalmani's *Khomeini, Sade and Me* won a PEN Translates award in 2015. Her translation of Ricardo Romero's novella *The President's Room* was published in 2017 and her translation of Colombian author Margarita García Robayo's work was published as the collection *Fish Soup* in 2018 by Charco Press. As well as translating literature, under the name of CMC Translations she provides transcreation, proofreading, and editing services on a daily basis for private clients and agencies.

Thank you all

for your support.

We do this for you,

and could not do

it without you.

DEAR SUBSCRIBERS,

We are both proud of and awed by what you've helped us accomplish so far in achieving and growing our mission. Since our founding, with your help, we've been able to reach over 100,000 English-language readers through the translation and publication of 32 award-winning books, from 5 continents, 24 countries, and 14 languages. In addition, we've been able to participate in over 50 programs in Dallas with 17 of our authors and translators and over 100 conversations nationwide reaching thousands of people, and were named Dallas's Best Publisher by *D Magazine*.

Deep Vellum is a 501c3 nonprofit literary arts organization founded in 2013 in Dallas's historic cultural neighborhood of Deep Ellum. Our mission is threefold: to cultivate a more vibrant, engaged literary arts community both locally and nationally; to promote the craft, discussion, and study of literary translation; and to publish award-winning, diverse international literature in English-language translations.

As a nonprofit organization, we rely on your generosity as individual donors, cultural organizations, government institutions, and charitable foundations. Your tax-deductible recurring or one-time donation provides the basis of our operational budget as we seek out and publish exciting literary works from around the globe and continue to build the partnerships that create a vibrant, thriving literary arts community. Deep Vellum offers various donor levels with opportunities to receive personalized benefits at each level, including books and Deep Vellum merchandise, invitations to special events, and recognition in each book and on our website.

In addition to donations, we rely on subscriptions from readers like you to provide the bedrock of our support, through an ongoing investment that demonstrates your commitment to our editorial vision and mission. The support our 5- and 10-book subscribers provide allows us to demonstrate to potential partners, bookstores, and organizations alike the support and demand for Deep Vellum's literature across a broad readership, giving us the ability to grow our mission in ever-new, ever-innovative ways.

It is crucial that English-language readers have access to diverse perspectives on the human experience, perspectives that literature is uniquely positioned to provide. You can keep the conversation going and growing with us by becoming involved as a donor, subscriber, or volunteer. Contact us at deepvellum.org to learn more today. We would love to hear from you.

Thank you all. Enjoy reading.

Will Evans
Founder & Publisher

PARTNERS

FIRST EDITION MEMBERSHIP
Anonymous (4)

TRANSLATOR'S CIRCLE

PRINTER'S PRESS MEMBERSHIP
Allred Capital Management
Ben & Sharon Fountain
Charles Dee Mitchell
David Tomlinson & Kathryn Berry
Judy Pollock
Loretta Siciliano
Lori Feathers
Mary Ann Thompson-Frenk & Joshua Frenk
Matthew Rittmayer
Meriwether Evans
Nick Storch
Pixel and Texel
Social Venture Partners Dallas
Stephen Bullock

AUTHOR'S LEAGUE
Farley Houston
Jacob Seifring
Lissa Dunlay
Stephen Bullock

PUBLISHER'S LEAGUE
Adam Rekerdres
Christie Tull
Justin Childress
Kay Cattarulla
KMGMT
Olga Kislova

EDITOR'S LEAGUE
Amrit Dhir
Brandon Kennedy
Garth Hallberg
Greg McConeghy
Linda Nell Evans
Mike Kaminsky
Patricia Storace
Steven Harding
Suejean Kim
Symphonic Source

READER'S LEAGUE
Caroline Casey
Chilton Thomson
Jeff Waxman
Marian Schwartz
Marlo D. Cruz Pagan

ADDITIONAL DONORS
Alan Shockley
Andrew Yorke
Anonymous (4)
Anthony Messenger
Bob & Katherine Penn
Bob Appel
Brandon Childress
Caitlin Baker
Charley Mitcherson
Cheryl Thompson
Cone Johnson
CS Maynard
Cullen Schaar
Daniel J. Hale
Dori Boone-Costantino
Ed Nawotka
Elizabeth Gillette
Ester & Matt Harrison
Grace Kenney
JJ Italiano
Kelly Falconer
Lea Courington
Leigh Ann Pike
Maaza Mengiste
Mark Haber
Mary Cline
Maynard Thomson
Michael Reklis
Mokhtar Ramadan
Nikki & Dennis Gibson
Patrick Kukucka
Patrick Kutcher
Rev. Elizabeth & Neil Moseley
Richard Meyer
Sherry Perry
Stephen Harding
Susan Carp
Susan Ernst
Theater Jones
Thomas DiPiero
Tim Perttula
Tony Thomson

SUBSCRIBERS

Ali Bolcakan
Andrew Bowles
Anita Tarar
Anonymous
Ben Nichols
Blair Bullock
Brandye Brown
Caitlin Schmid
Caroline West
Charles Dee Mitchell
Chris McCann
Chris Mullikin
Chris Sweet
Christie Tull
Courtney Sheedy
Daniel Kushner
David Bristow
David Tomlinson & Kathryn Berry
David Travis
Elizabeth Johnson
Ellen Miller
Farley Houston
Florence Lopez
Hannah McGinty
Holly LaFon
Jason Linden
Jeff Goldberg
Joe Maceda
John Schmerein
John Winkelman
Erin Crossett
Joshua Edwin
Kelly Baxter
Kenneth McClain
Kevin Winter
Lesley Conzelman
Lora Lafayette
Lytton Smith
Mario Sifuentez
Marisa Bhargava
Martha Gifford
Mary Brockson
Matt Cheney
Michael Aguilar
Michael Elliott
Mies de Vries
Nathan Wey
Neal Chuang
Nicholas R. Theis
Patrick Shirak
Reid Allison
Robert Keefe
Ronald Morton
Shelby Vincent
Stephanie Barr
Steve Jansen
Todd Crocken
Todd Jailer
Wenyang Chen
Will Pepple
William Fletcher

AVAILABLE NOW FROM DEEP VELLUM

MICHÈLE AUDIN · *One Hundred Twenty-One Days*
translated by Christiana Hills · FRANCE

EDUARDO BERTI · *The Imagined Land*
translated by Charlotte Coombe · ARGENTINA

CARMEN BOULLOSA · *Texas: The Great Theft* · *Before* · *Heavens on Earth*
translated by Samantha Schnee · Peter Bush · Shelby Vincent · MEXICO

LEILA S. CHUDORI · *Home*
translated by John H. McGlynn · INDONESIA

SARAH CLEAVE · *Banthology: Stories from Banned Nations*

ANANDA DEVI · *Eve Out of Her Ruins*
translated by Jeffrey Zuckerman · MAURITIUS

ALISA GANIEVA · *Bride and Groom* · *The Mountain and the Wall*
translated by Carol Apollonio · RUSSIA

ANNE GARRÉTA · *Sphinx* · *Not One Day*
translated by Emma Ramadan · FRANCE

JÓN GNARR · *The Indian* · *The Pirate* · *The Outlaw*
translated by Lytton Smith · ICELAND

NOEMI JAFFE · *What are the Blind Men Dreaming?*
translated by Julia Sanches & Ellen Elias-Bursac · BRAZIL

CLAUDIA SALAZAR JIMÉNEZ · *Blood of the Dawn*
translated by Elizabeth Bryer · PERU

JOSEFINE KLOUGART · *Of Darkness*
translated by Martin Aitken · DENMARK

YANICK LAHENS · *Moonbath*
translated by Emily Gogolak · HAITI

JUNG YOUNG MOON · *Vaseline Buddha*
translated by Yewon Jung · SOUTH KOREA

FOUAD LAROUI · *The Curious Case of Dassoukine's Trousers*
translated by Emma Ramadan · MOROCCO

LINA MERUANE · *Seeing Red*
translated by Megan McDowell · CHILE

FISTON MWANZA MUJILA · *Tram 83*
translated by Roland Glasser · DEMOCRATIC REPUBLIC OF CONGO

ILJA LEONARD PFEIJFFER · *La Superba*
translated by Michele Hutchison · NETHERLANDS

RICARDO PIGLIA · *Target in the Night*
translated by Sergio Waisman · ARGENTINA

SERGIO PITOL · *The Art of Flight* · *The Journey* · *The Magician of Vienna*
translated by George Henson · MEXICO

EDUARDO RABASA · *A Zero-Sum Game*
translated by Christina MacSweeney · MEXICO

MIKHAIL SHISHKIN · *Calligraphy Lesson: The Collected Stories*
translated by Marian Schwartz, Leo Shtutin, Mariya Bashkatova, Sylvia Maizell · RUSSIA

BAE SUAH · *Recitation*
translated by Deborah Smith · SOUTH KOREA

JUAN RULFO · *The Golden Cockerel & Other Writings*
translated by Douglas J. Weatherford · MEXICO

SERHIY ZHADAN · *Voroshilovgrad*
translated by Reilly Costigan-Humes & Isaac Stackhouse Wheeler · UKRAINE

FORTHCOMING FROM DEEP VELLUM

MARIA GABRIELA LLANSOL · *The Geography of Rebels Trilogy: The Book of Communities; The Remaining Life; In the House of July & August*
translated by Audrey Young · PORTUGAL

BRICE MATTHIEUSSENT · *Revenge of the Translator*
translated by Emma Ramadan · FRANCE

SERGIO PITOL · *Mephisto's Waltz: Selected Short Stories*
translated by George Henson · MEXICO

ZAHIA RAHMANI · *"Muslim": A Novel*
translated by Matthew Reeck · FRANCE/ALGERIA

PABLO MARTÍN SÁNCHEZ · *The Anarchist Who Shared My Name*
translated by Jeff Diteman · SPAIN

ÓFEIGUR SIGURÐSSON · *Öræfi: The Wasteland*
translated by Lytton Smith · ICELAND

KIM YIDEUM · *Blood Sisters*
translated by Ji yoon Lee · SOUTH KOREA